EXTREME
ELVIN

ALSO BY CHRIS LYNCH

CHRIS LYNCH

EXTREME ELVIN

HarperCollinsPublishers

Extreme Elvin
Copyright © 1999 by Chris Lynch
For information address HarperCollins Children's Books, a division of
HarperCollins Publishers, 10 East 53rd Street, New York, NY 10022.

Library of Congress Cataloging-in-Publication Data
Lynch, Chris.
    Extreme Elvin / Chris Lynch.
        p.   cm.
    Sequel to: Slot machine.
    Summary: As he enters high school, fourteen-year-old Elvin continues to
deal with his weight problem as he tries to find his place among his peers.
    ISBN 0-06-028040-9. — ISBN 0-06-028210-X (lib. bdg.)
    [1. Weight control—Fiction.   2. Self-acceptance—Fiction.   3. High
schools—Fiction.   4. Schools—Fiction.]   I. Title.
PZ7.L979739Ex   1998   98-28820
[Fic]—dc21   CIP
                                                                                          AC

Typography by Alison Donalty
1   2   3   4   5   6   7   8   9   10
❖
First Edition

Visit us on the World Wide Web!
http://www.harperchildrens.com

THIS BOOK IS FOR

WALKER AND SOPHIA

CONTENTS

THE ORIGINAL EQUIPMENT

So, how many relationships is a person supposed to be able to manage anyway?

And that's the first thing right there, isn't it? *Relationships*. Hell. I never had any relationships before I hit fourteen.

But now I'm fourteen. Everything changes. Even the language. Now I'm high school age. *Teen*. Cripes. I was, technically, a teen when I was thirteen, because I could hear it in there—thir*teen*, see—but apparently that was different. I was really thireen. Now I'm A Teen. Very different animal, apparently. Young adult. You know *that* one was dreamed up by an old adult. All I know is nobody consulted me.

I used to have a mother, and a friend, and another friend, and . . . well that's about it. Now I got relationships.

Still have Mom. She's cool. Quick with a joke and to light up my smoke and all that. Sometimes a little nutty, sure, but she is the best in the world at her version of the mom thing. Of course, I don't think anybody else practices her version of the mom thing, so she's got very little competition. If I could manage having more than two friends, it is possible I'd give her the third slot. But don't repeat that.

Still got the two, though. The original equipment. Could do better, probably, but I'm lazy is what it is. That's why I've had the same two friends forever. Friend One, Mikie. Friend One-A, Frankie. Been through everything together. Kid stuff mostly, but it seemed like a lot at the time.

Who'm I kidding? It seems like a lot now, too.

And the kid stuff held together, even when it started looking like we weren't going to get to be kids anymore. We were like one organism, the three of us, as we went from grade school to high school, never actually talking about it, never mentioning the hundreds of choices available across the city. Don't know who decided on this joint first, but here we are, again in the same place, with no evidence of who followed whom.

Then there was even this little summer test camp for us, to break us . . . break us *in*, I mean . . . before we actually came to school in September. It was kind of a horror show that taught us a lot about what to look out for in the next four years but really, in the end, turned out to be more about *us*—me, Mikie, and Frankie—with a lot of other players shuffling in and out of the game.

That's a thing right there. Other players shuffling in. Seems like it can't be simple anymore. And for the first time ever, I know I don't want it to be.

Which brings me to the one more thing, and brings me to now. Relationships. What happens to what you've got, when you get all this more?

"Why are you sitting like that, Elvin? Sit up straight."

"What?" I sat up straight. Straight hurt. I leaned a little to one side again. "What, Ma? Sitting like *what*? I'm sitting fine. Maybe I'm up straight and *you're* slanted."

She continued slicing perfect banana coins onto my Special K from over my shoulder, then went to the counter and came back with a saucer. On the saucer were seven apricots arranged in a circle around the center ring. A beautiful overripe apricot-blossom flower.

"I'm not eating those, you know." I looked so I was viewing her face-on and serious—and upside down and backward. "I don't care if you arrange them in the shape of flowers, or animals, or airplanes . . . you can even shape them like *food* if you want. . . ."

"You know, if there is something making you sit sideways like that, it probably would be good to tell me." Would that be a smile on my ma's face? Yes, I believe it would.

Oh, she heard me all right. She was well aware that I wanted to talk about something else. She's fairly brilliant at playing a kind of verbal kung fu with me when she wants to talk and I don't. Fortunately, I, and only I, am more than a match for her.

"I said, no apricots, lady. Take them away."

"You love apricots."

"Maybe I do, maybe I don't. All I'm saying is, I'm not having them." I straightened up, picked up the saucer, and balanced it on the tips of my fingers, waiting for her to come up from behind and take it away.

She came up from behind, took one off the plate, and tucked it neatly into my mouth before I could react. I've got to stop leaving my mouth hanging open all the time.

"Maaa," I said quite clearly and angrily even though I was chewing. Everything sounds like *maaa* when you're chewing.

"I'm sorry, but you know how it works: If you want bananas, or cheese, or anything binding . . ."

I swallowed the thing without even chewing sufficiently. "All, right, all right, I think that's enough—"

"For god's sake, Elvin, we're both adults here—"

"Oh, is that it? This is what I've been waiting for all these years? This is what adults talk about that I could never hear before? *Binding*? Jeez, if I knew this, I would have grown up a lot quicker."

See, now, if nobody intervened, this could go on forever. Because this is the key to Bishop family communication: *Not*. Not, is the key. With my mother and myself only one of us at a time ever seems to want to get at something. So it's a tail-chasing competition of one of us asking questions and the other thinking up clever and thrilling ways of not answering the questions.

Except, in the end, we always seem to have gotten at something, somehow.

She sat down across from me. "Why are you sitting that way?" she asked as she chewed a knuckle.

"Fine, Ma," I said, pushing my cereal bowl away. "Take the bananas. Just take 'em."

"Are you injured?"

Thank god Frankie screamed for me from the sidewalk.

"Gotta run, Ma. Go ahead and finish my apricots for me."

"We're going to talk about this later, Elvin."

I kissed my mother on the cheek. "That'll be swell."

"Don't kiss me on the cheek. And don't say swell to me ever again or I'll wash your mouth out with Mr. Clean."

No dope, my ma. She knows when she's being mocked.

"Look at the way you're walking," she said as she watched me from behind. "What kind of walk is that?"

I ran.

"What kind of walk is that?" Mikie asked as he and Frankie watched me approach.

"What is it with everybody today, I gotta have a name for my walk? Okay, this is my Tuesday kind of walk."

"No, there's something wrong with you," Frankie said, as we headed down the block toward the bus stop.

"Listen, I just finished getting tough with my ma. You want a piece of that, huh?" I sounded so tough I was scaring myself. It was the affliction getting to me.

I was the only one I was scaring though. The boys persisted. They are persistent boys. Like I said, they have been my friends forever, and being my friend brings along with it an urge to fix me. I'm a fixer-upper, and these guys are show houses.

I hate 'em.

Just kidding.

But if I did hate 'em, you couldn't blame me. Frankie's handsome like a Greek statue only with more color and mouth and hair. And he's got this oozy charm thing that would make you sick if you could resist it, which nobody seems able to do. And Mikie—whom we call Dad because he's so mature and sensible and all that crap—is, like, the guy who fits in every picture. He could fit, for example, with the poindexter crowd, hang around and talk with them and not fall on his face even though he's got no poindexter in him. He could then walk away from that bunch, head into the gym, and join any pickup game of basketball that might be going on. He doesn't dominate a game, but he's always a *player*. Never picked lower than third. There have been times when he was picked twice, once by each team, while I was still sitting there totally, embarrassingly, available in the talent pool.

Lofty figures, you might say. So what are they doing with a benchwarmer like me?

Because. I got to them before the world did. So they are different to me.

Which doesn't mean they still don't want to fix me from time to time.

"Give it up," Mikie said. "You're among friends. If you can't tell us . . ."

I paused, winced, looked in every direction, including the sky for eavesdropping UFOs, then I whispered its name to my nearest and dearest.

"*Hemorrhoids?*" Frankie squealed. His immediate reaction was amused; then he got all philosophical, trying to work this out. "How do they know who to go to? I mean, like, hemorrhoids and bald spots and lazy eyes and stuff. They never go to somebody like me. They always go to . . ."

"Shut up," I snapped. Understand, if he was *trying* to insult me, I wouldn't have been so upset.

"It is kind of funny, El," Mike said.

"It is kind of *not*," I replied.

"Come on," Mike tried again. "Don't make a big thing. You're always exaggerating. It's not really, really painful, right?"

Which explained it. Mike is a very sympathetic soul—who was a little short on information at the moment.

"No, it doesn't hurt much, Mike," I said. "Run and find me a tree branch that's on fire, and I'll show ya."

"What're you doing with hemorrhoids?" Frank asked, still talking really loudly.

"What am I *doing* with them, Frank? What am I *doing* with them? Oh, well, I'm doing what everybody does with them. They're like a hobby, y'know. Like being a Trekkie or a marble collector or something. We go to conventions and stuff and compare. 'Say, whatcha got there?' 'Oh, I got a couple aggies and a pinkie and a big ol' cat's eye. Ain't she a beaut.' That's what I'm doing with them, Frank."

Mikie squirmed, winced. *Now*, he got it. Frank gave me a disgusted look.

We mounted the bus and, as usual, Frank left us and went straight to the back to hook up with his boys. He could still spend some of his time with us, as long as he paid due attention to the licking of appropriate boots, and having his own licked by kids even more popularity-conscious than himself. Frankie was in a different social slot from me and Mike now. Earned himself some stripes. After the school's summer camp, he was a made man, and made a big deal out of it.

I was there, though.

And I'll keep my Mr. Nobody social rating, thanks anyway.

Mikie and I slipped into seats midway down, joining the rabble. We sat across the aisle from each other. There was somebody taking up every window seat.

"So what are you gonna do about it?" he asked discreetly.

"First thing I'm gonna do is I'm gonna ask you to take that look off your face," I said.

He looked like he was sitting in a bathtub filled with cold potato-leek soup.

"It's *my* affliction, remember? I'll make the faces." I made one. "I don't know what I'm gonna do," I whined.

Mikie shook his head thoughtfully. "You know what everyone's gonna say, right? You know what they always say at a school like ours, when a guy gets—"

"I know." I buried my face in my hands.

"Gonna say you're easy—"

"I said I know, Mike . . ."

"Volunteer center on the football team . . . captain of the shower squad . . . good ol' Elvin, Just Say *Go* . . ."

"All right, I know, I know. I read the walls like everybody else. But I really don't need that kind of popularity."

"I don't know," he said. "You could use *some* kind. . . ."

I opened my hands, and my face, to my good friend. "And you're the guy who's *helping* me, is that right?"

"So what? A little bit of a rep would do you some good. At least your phone will finally start ringing."

"Hey. It rings plenty, all right."

"Ya. For your mom."

I went all dark on him. It's quite a sight. The whole thing, glowering, scowling, growling, snarling.

"Thought we had a rule?"

"That wasn't a mother joke."

"It was a mother joke."

"No. If it's true, it doesn't qualify as a mother joke."

Hmmm. "Well it's damn close to a mother joke."

"You know, El, I been meaning to bring this up anyway. We made that rule when we were, what, seven? Don't you think . . . ?"

"It's a perfectly good rule," I snapped. "It's a time-less rule, one that'll make sense when we're fifty."

"If you're still having this discussion when we are fifty . . . about how nobody can joke about your mom and all . . . then you're going to be having the discussion *alone*."

"I don't know why we're talking about that anyway. I'm not going to see fifty. I'm not going to see October, Mike."

"I don't think it can kill ya, El."

I didn't answer. Maybe I wasn't going to die, but it would have been nice to be treated like I was. That kind of thing was Mikie's job. I waited.

"Hurts though, huh?" he said somberly.

I nodded bravely. Felt better.

"Kinky, no?" Frankie said, which is what I'd expect Frankie to say. We were sitting around my kitchen table after school, discussing the assembly we'd sat through earlier in the day. Eating graham crackers with peanut butter. And milk. A good wholesome snack, even with Frank kinking things up.

I like that they call it Assembly. It gives me pictures in my head. Like, we're all so mangled and disarranged that they have to convey the whole lot of us down to the gym and put us back together again.

And what did they assemble us for, on this otherwise fine September day? To tell us about the sister school.

We have a sister school.

Does she look like us? Will she wash the dishes? Does she have any nice-looking friends we could meet?

No. We dance with this sister.

Should I be confused here? Should I be ashamed of the thoughts that may be dancing in my head? Excited, though, is what I am. Excited in the most unpleasant, terrified way, at the mention of dancing with the sister school. Thank god I don't have a real sister, if this is the way I respond to . . .

"Why do we have to have a sister school?" I asked. "And why do we have to dance with it?"

"Because," Mikie said, "you may have noticed, we're all guys at our school."

"Hey, I take gym like everybody else. I noticed."

"Well now they're gonna fill that gym up with girls, and I for one think it's a fine idea," Frankie said.

The school did this every year, apparently. Got all us oozy pimply-faced frosh guys together with the pimply-faced frosh girls of our sister school, St. Theresa's, to stir us up with forty-year-old doo-wop music and Chips Ahoy cookies and see what kind of sexual slaw we could make of ourselves.

"Yes, a very fine idea," said my mother, walking in from work.

"Yes, well, nobody asked you," I said. Bratty. I get like that now that I'm in high school.

"Wait till I tell your father," she snapped back at me.

That would be my dead father.

Mikie and Frankie stopped chewing and stared at me.

■■

"Ma, could you stop the talking to dead people thing? At least while we have company? I have few enough friends as it is."

"What company?" she pointed out—reasonably enough. "We don't have company, we have *them*."

"Well maybe if we practice on these two we can get some real company eventually."

She plunked herself down into the fourth kitchen chair, leaned forward on her elbows real friendly like. She smiled at Mikie, who smiled back. She smiled at Frankie, who took that as his cue to do something with his feet under the table that made her kick him. This was kind of an ongoing story, and neither one of them seemed particularly fazed by it.

"So, Elvin," she said. "Are we ready to discuss your problem?"

"Ah, *hell*," I said as both of my friends got up and walked out.

"You two probably want to be alone," Mike said, rustling Frank out.

"Can we hang outside the window?" Frankie asked before Mikie gave him one final mighty shove.

Now that we were alone . . . I bolted from the table, locked myself in the bathroom and ran myself a steaming—and noisy—bath.

BIG AND TALL

The three of us were standing in the mall parking lot, looking up at the big sign.

At the big, and tall, sign.

"I have my limit," I said sternly.

"Ya, I'd say your limit's about two sixty these days, Elvin," Frank cracked.

"I don't care if it's *three* sixty, I am not buying clothes in there. No sir. Anyway, what do I need new clothes for? The clothes I have are fine. I look great in my clothes."

Mikie got very serious with me. He put his hand on my shoulder. "Elvin, I am your friend. I am your friend, but even I wouldn't say—"

"Shut up," I said. "Did my mother put you up to this?"

"Elvin, you are never going to get anywhere with the girls if you don't spiff up your look a little," Frank said.

"And I think you should stop mentioning your mother every other sentence. Nobody wants to date Principal Skinner."

"I told you already, I'll be spiffy enough when my diet kicks in. I can feel it working already. Whoa, there it is now. Feel that? It's kicking."

"That's good," Mike said. He was doing the serious thing again, which somehow was even more degrading than Frankie's ridicule thing. See, when Frankie abused and humiliated me, it was half accidental, because he was teaching me life in his style, and his style was mayhem. But when Mikie did it, he was being Dad. He was always right, and we all knew it. If Mikie was bringing me down, I always assumed down was where I belonged.

"Maybe you wouldn't have the 'rhoids if you'd keep the weight under control. . . ."

See? Like that.

"So what. You guys can stop worrying about my health, and we can skip the Big and Tall Shop because since my diet started this morning I've already gotten everything under control. So let's skip the clothes store and go on over and spend the money at Pizzeria Uno instead."

"Come on, El, the dance is Friday. You can't lose that much by then, and I am determined to get you some companionship if it kills me," Frankie said.

And you thought he couldn't be nice.

"We can't change you," he added, "but we might be able to disguise you, with the right outfit."

Never mind.

I looked up at the sign again. I closed my eyes tight.

I opened them again. It was still there. It was still big and tall.

"I can't do it. This is the lowest, you know? Do you understand, what I am admitting, if I start buying my clothes in there? Huh? Do ya?"

They looked at each other, then looked back at me.

"Uh-huh," they both said.

So. See these are the things here at fourteen long hard years, the things I have to reassess. Are these guys my friends, my best-of-alls, because they are the people who will tell me the truth? Or would they be better for me if they could just make me feel good by saying whatever necessary? Y'know, every part of me, every cell, every jiggly cell, wants to tell them to shut up, beat it boys, leave me alone. Two problems with that, though. First, they probably wouldn't listen to me if I did tell them to blow. Second, then again they might.

That still doesn't mean I was ready to take this thing head-on.

"Well, no sale," I said. "I can't do it. I can't admit that."

So there we were. Two well-proportioned high school freshmen and myself, standing outside the B&T, staring.

"You're tall," Mikie said suddenly.

"Huh?" I asked.

"Huh?" Frank asked.

"You're tall, Elvin," Mike repeated. "You had a growth spurt recently or something? Because I didn't realize before this how *tall* you are. Isn't that right, Franko?"

Franko was a little slow on the uptake. "Tall? I suppose, he's maybe kinda tall. Where we goin' with this?"

"*Tall*, Frank. He's tall. He's wicked tall." Mikie was gesturing madly up at the Big and Tall sign as he spoke, trying to get the point over.

As a thinker, Frank is a very handsome guy. But eventually he got it. "Ah," Frank said, "*tall*. You been drinking giraffe milk, El? Listen, we got to get you into the Big and *Tall* shop, get you outfitted. . . ."

We had magically gotten to that place where a person's life becomes so pathetic it isn't even embarrassing anymore. I was enjoying it.

I allowed myself to be tugged toward the shop, each friend pulling one of my hands.

"I better duck on the way in," I said as Mikie held the glass door open for me.

"Better pull on your boots too," Frank said. "It's gettin' deep."

Mike elbowed him in the chest.

"Yes sir, what can I show you?" the very big and not so tall salesguy said. To me.

I frowned at him. "How do you know it's me? There are three of us just walked in, so how come you came right up to me, huh?"

The guy flinched. Then he looked at Mikie, who got way up on his toes, pointed at me, smiled and nodded at the guy. Frank, who was about three inches taller than me, slouched dramatically and gave the guy the high sign.

Good friends. Knuckleheads, but good friends.

"Oh, well, you're the *tall* guy," the salesman said to me. "Obviously."

I suppose he'd served a neurotic defensive fatty or two in his career.

"He'd like to see some of your finest tall-people pants, please," Mikie said.

The salesman looked at my waist. "Thirty-eight, right, Stretch?"

"You got it, cowboy," I said, and we followed him to the racks.

It was a pretty silly scene, actually. Mike would select a shirt and Frank would select the pants to match, nobody would ask me anything, and then I'd try on whatever they pushed on me. "Right this way," the salesman said; then he'd shove me into a snug-fitting dressing room where I'd wrestle with the ensemble, trying to get it on and get a look at myself in the mirror that was practically rubbing up against me and trying not to expose the glory of me too soon as the skimpy curtain that served as a door insisted on attaching itself to me with all its static clingy might.

I know, by the way, that they do hide surveillance cameras in dressing rooms. It's against the law and all, but we all know they do it. And it's not to catch shoplifters half as much as it is to catch scenes like this one. I'd do it if I were them.

"Come out," Mikie called the *first* time I took twenty minutes with an outfit.

"Cripes," he said when I came out wearing my own clothes. "What the hell, El?"

I mumbled. "Try thirty-nine."

"Jeez," Frankie said. "Whatja do, Elvin, bring snacks in there with ya?"

I retained all my dignity. Fortunately this didn't take long since I didn't bring all that much with me in the first place. "Thirty . . . nine, please."

"There should be a law," Frank grumbled, snatching the pants away from me. Frank takes fashion issues very seriously. "If your waist number is bigger than your inseam number, you should be forced to wear corduroys that thigh-whistle at you every day till you get your act together."

I didn't have to take that kind of crap off him. There are moments in life when even us even-tempered guys have to spout. This was one of those moments. This was where I needed to draw a line. When the going gets tough and all that, right?

Right?

"And bring me back a Coke," I yelled.

That would have been funny, huh? If I were trying to make a joke instead of a stand.

It was a real boys' day out though. I tried on seventeen combinations without even counting the hats and socks. The guys were very patient with me.

"Cripes, Elvin, just wear a toga," Frank said.

"Hang in there five more minutes, Elvin," Mike cracked, "and that outfit will qualify as secondhand and you'll get it cheaper."

"Five more minutes and you'll owe me rent," the salesman snapped.

"Sheesh," I said. "What a grouch. Maybe a year from now when I buy my *next* new outfit I'll take my business somewhere else."

"If you're even out of the dressing room by then," he said.

"Hey, wait a minute," Mikie said. "They're wheeling in the spring collection. A whole season changed while you were in there. New colors, new fabrics."

Can't believe I fell for it. I stuck my head out through the curtain again, and they nabbed me. Frank grabbed my head, Mikie ran into the dressing room and collected all my old clothes, shoes, everything, and the salesman led the group of us to the register.

"He'll take this," somebody said, the voice muffled by the arm around my head.

But they were right. I looked smashing. Once I got my shoes on I was a new man, and all I wanted to do was parade around that mall and check myself out in every store window. The shirt was one of those granddad things, with about a hundred buttons running between the straight-up collar and the navel, where the button deal stopped entirely. A button-down shirt that you still have to pull over head! Madness. Fashion genius. I could feel everybody looking at me, and well they should, with that one subtle-but-daring powder-blue stripe running between each pair of brown stripes. Imagine!

And brown jeans. You heard me. Brown. I looked at my reflection in the Puppy Palace and had to just shake my head. Brown jeans. Not the basic boring blue jeans. Not even the now-clichéd black jeans. Even the drug-addicted dogs of Puppy Palace sat up and took notice. Right, well they didn't sit up exactly, not all the way up, but their heads lifted, a couple of them, with the drool making wood shavings stick to their chins like little goat beards.

Maybe somebody would buy them, finally, if they were disguised as goats.

Even the hopeless basset hound—who had been sitting right there in that front window since the mall opened in 1987, who couldn't even *remember* being a puppy (and judging from his glassy eyes couldn't remember this morning), who had been reduced to fifteen dollars *with* a coupon for a ten-pound bag of dry dog food—even he dragged himself closer to the glass and checked me out. I read his floppy brown felt lips.

"Wow," the basset hound said.

Then he fell over dead. Finally, mercifully, dead. I killed him.

That, ladies and gentlemen, is a fashion statement.

"Oh, he is not dead, ya jerk," Frankie said as he walked on ahead. "He always sleeps like that."

Mikie went up close to the glass. "I don't know,

Franko. His nose is pressed right up to the window, and he's not fogging it."

"He hasn't been able to fog the glass since that little girl dropped him at the sidewalk sale."

"Maybe if he's dead," Mike mused, "we could go in and see if they'll let us have him for a fiver. The bag of food is worth that much, and I can bring that home to feed to Freckles, my hamster, for the rest of his life."

Frankie laughed. Obviously these guys were not as tuned as I to the bigness of this moment. I had just gone from portly ragbag to Killer Joe Ladyslayer in one afternoon. The dance was two days away, and I didn't even want to go to sleep until then. I picked up the pace and led the boys on a few brisk laps of the mall. We looked like one of those old-dude mallwalker exercise clubs.

"I can't wait for the Ball now."

"The *Ball*?" they both yiked at once.

"Elvin, calm thyself, all right?" Mike said. "This isn't a ball. It's not even a real dance, really. It's like . . . a lab exercise. Almost like a cross between an extra gym class and a social skills seminar."

"It's for scouting reports, really," Franko said. "So they can tell right off the bat who they gotta keep tabs on." He put his fists on his narrow hips and looked me and Mikie up and down. "You guys are safe. But they're gonna make me wear one of those electronic monitor ankle bracelets for the whole year once they see me dance."

I've seen him dance. Without a girl, even. Saw him

in his basement, demonstrating moves with a full-length mirror reflective version of himself. He *should* wear one of those anklets. He should wear one on *each* ankle. And they should be linked together with a sturdy little chain.

"But it's so stupid," I said. "They're having it Friday afternoon. It won't even be dark by the time it's over. How much trouble could we get into?"

Frankie's eyes went big and bug on me. I was such a challenge for him that he often couldn't decide whether to get angry at me or pity me. Usually he managed both. "God, are you *ever* gonna grow up to life's possibilities, El? Bring a notebook and watch me closely."

I didn't care if it was a practice dance to grade us on social skills, or a lab experiment to flush out the Frankie among us, or an extra gym class slipped into the schedule. As long as I got to glide into my new duds and lay the new-model Elvin on a batch of captive girl folk.

Might be nice, after all, to get a close-up look at some girls when there was a chance they might actually look back. I felt half stupid for paying so much attention to how I looked, because that was so not me. But at the moment I wanted a little more than just me. Was that something to apologize for?

No. Full steam ahead. I wore the clothes for the rest of Wednesday afternoon. Put them on again to wear around the house for an hour before school on Thursday. Put them right back on when I got home that afternoon. I was primed. The clothes *do* make the man, and they made me into Mr. Slickmaster.

I was so confident I forgot all about my diet. Who needs a diet when you're Mr. Slickmaster?

"Oh my *god*," I yelled first thing Friday morning. *The* Friday morning. Dance Friday. Good Friday, Great Friday.

Fat Friday.

"No, no, no!" I yelled at myself in that desperate, deathly wheezy voice a person makes when he tries to suck in his stomach and scream at himself at the same time.

"Suck!" I yelled.

"Elvin Bishop," my mother yelled back, from outside my bedroom door.

"Not the swear suck, Ma, the command Suck!" I explained more calmly. "I'm talking to my stomach. It grew. Ma, it grew, just since last night. Out of no place. Like the virgin birth."

I yanked. I fell back on the bed. I pulled. You know the method, right? Grab a fistful of material with your right hand and try to haul the button across the great plains over to the other side where your left fist is cattle-driving the buttonhole over to meet it. But what you really do is wind up torquing yourself all over the place like a washing machine.

I looked just like one of those sexy ads with the models pulling on shrink-to-fits by standing on their heads and writhing on satin sheets and . . . you know.

Just like that.

"Suck!"

"Elvin, that is enough."

"Poof, Ma. Just like that. Out of nowhere. Just since last night."

"Out of nowhere? Virgin birth? Just since last night? Just since the pot roast, you mean? And since the cherry pie with ice cream, and the yogurt-covered raisins?" She was fully in the room now, bold and uninvited. I was lying flat on my back on the floor staring up at her with my pants still undone. "Or since the *second* round of the pot roast? Followed by a repeat of all of the above?"

I sighed. "Wouldja get to the point, Ma? I kind of have a lot on my plate today."

"Self-control, I suppose would be my point, *Son*."

"Fine, point taken. Now would you just step on my abdomen with both feet while I . . . you know, like with luggage."

"How could you do this to yourself? I told you to slow down—"

"Stress. I've been under a lot of—"

"Put on the blue pants, for godsake."

"I will *not* put on the blue bus-driver pants. I am not a bus driver. I will not *be* a bus driver. Bus drivers wear their pants fastened *above* the waistline, or *below* the waistline, but Elvin Bishop wears his waistline *at* the waistline. No. I'm almost there now . . . just another . . ."

"I can't watch this."

"I hadn't meant to perform it yet for a live audience anyway. Please close the door on your way out."

She did.

24

"Suck!"

I heard the doorbell ring.

"Suck!"

I could not believe how fast those two rats got up the stairs and into my room.

"Since Wednesday, El?" Mikie asked, staring at my stomach like he was my doctor watching my heart monitor flatline.

"So kill me," I snarled. "I baked a banana bread yesterday afternoon. I can't leave the baking to my mother, because she cannot bake. Do I leave her to starve to death then, my own mother, just so I can get a girl?"

Yes, I could hear what I sounded like. And yes, what I was really trying to say was that I felt like I did the day I played football at camp and got my head slapped until my nose bled. I sort of cried that time, but I sort of would *not* now. Big difference, you know, when you've been the one slapping your own head. With a pot roast.

I was thrashing around the room pretty good now, trying to get these pants to close.

"Better watch it, man," Frankie said. "Remember your condition. My grandmother had the 'rhoids, and every time she got worked up she had a flare-up. The time she found my private stack of magazines, she had to eat standing up at the sink for almost a month."

"What about the blue pants?" Mikie suggested.

"Shut up with the blue pants, all right? Go downstairs and have breakfast with my mother."

25

"Listen then," Frank said, checking his watch. "Don't button the pants. Hold them closed with the belt, and keep the granddad shirt untucked to cover it up."

I had managed to get up to standing position by then. But those words brought me back down onto the bed. I unpuffed my chest, repuffed my stomach, and sat with my face in my hands. "Ah. So I'm back to the tent maneuver. What a disgrace."

"So what. At least this way you still get to wear the new gear, and if you control yourself for a few hours, you can try again after lunch."

When I showed no sign of life, Mikie hit me with his own version of defibrillator paddles.

"We can do this, Elvin."

We. You heard it.

I sucked it in, I sucked it up, I held the tent maneuver, and I would control myself.

As we walked to the bus stop, Frankie was already into the next stage of my development. It didn't seem to matter to him that with me gaining girth at the rate of two stomach inches per twelve hours, I'd never get a girl to look at me outside a circus. He was already working on what I was going to do with this girl once I got her.

"Dinners are good," he said, "but don't go Mexican. Flowers are good. Candy is good, but creams, not caramels. She'd be, like, picking stuff out of her teeth the whole time . . . and no bowling. Bowling's cool, but kind of . . . wait, check that." Frank got a glassy faraway look.

He's a visualizer. Visualizing a bowling date, apparently. "Do. Do take her bowling. . . ."

Then it hit me.

"Wait!" I said, spun, and ran back toward home.

"What are you doing, El?" Mike called. "You're going to be late."

But it didn't matter. I was already sweating, chugging, steaming my way home even though the bus was only five minutes away.

I burst through the kitchen door, found my mother finishing the last of her coffee.

"Did you wash my pants while I was sleeping?" I demanded.

It is very hard to unsettle my mother.

She took another sip. "Of course I did. You wore them for two days, and today was the dance—"

"Ahhhh," I said. "Ahhh. You shrunk my pants. You shrunk my pants." I made a move to the door. Turned back to her. "You shrunk my pants."

"Your needle is skipping, son."

"Huh?" I turned to the door again. "My needle?"

"It's an old album joke. Never mind."

"You shrunk my pants. Then you let me believe . . ."

"The fact remains, you ate atrociously."

"The bus. I'm gonna be late." I threw the door open and ran out. I'd sweat myself into those pants yet. I would not be denied, whether my own mother was subconsciously trying to sabotage me or not.

I ran back in, kissed Ma on the cheek, ran out again.

The bus, and my friends, were long gone by the time I got to the stop.

Oh well, as long as I was at it . . .

It was a three-mile run. Well, it was a three-quarter-mile run, followed by a one-mile walk, followed by a half-mile run, followed by a half-mile walk with a side cramp for company, followed by a very very sweaty quarter-mile run. If you had asked me whether any of that was possible before now, I'd have bet against me.

But I made it. I made it on my own. I made it with my pants buttoned (sweat-to-fit stretch-to-fit denims). Didn't even matter that I made it twenty-five minutes late.

Didn't matter to me, anyway. The late lady slid open her glass partition and was already making out a slip for me when I laid myself out on her desktop.

"Latelady, you're not really going to give me detention, are you?"

"Sure I am," she said with a smile. She's not mean, really, just enjoys her job. Everybody who's not late likes her.

"But I ran. Look at me. You can see that I ran."

"Maybe not. Maybe you swam."

"No, listen. You don't understand. I've got a story."

"Oh a *story*. You've got a *story*. Well, that's a horse of a different color then, isn't it? Most of the tardies don't have stories. Come in, come in."

Latelady likes sarcasm. And she winked at me. Like she knew everything.

It was all over with that wink.

"But it's Friday," I pleaded. "I'm a freshman. I'm going to the dance." In my dripping sweaty delirium, I really expected her to understand. Latelady was, after all, a lady. Somewhere in my world I have always understood that ladies understood. That they were . . . I don't know, more willing to appreciate the sap running through a guy like me. That's why I wanted to get to know more of them, starting with *this* very afternoon. That's why I was sweating, after all, because this was very important, this dance, and Latelady had to know that, had to know it.

"Here's your dance card," she said, handing me my detention slip.

FIGHT OR FLIGHT? DUH.

There were two of us in detention that day. Me, and Metzger. Metzger was an acquaintance from my brief career as a wrestler at camp. That fell right after my football/head slap/nosebleed period, and before my stint in the priesthood reserves. Have I mentioned how much the school's introductory camp helped prepare me for the real world?

Anyway, Metzger. He kind of held a grudge from one time when I gouged him and bit him and stuff before I knew the wrestling rules. I had retired, but ol' Metz kept trying to coax me out of retirement every time I saw him.

Fortunately detention at our school was a fairly loose business, and as long as you showed up, the monitor left you alone. The monitor was a rotating deal of different teachers, and nobody knows how the assignments get made. Judging by how thrilled the teacher always is to be there, it's safe to assume that detention monitor acts as a sort of teacher detention system, probably for offenses like eating the last donut in the faculty lounge or showing up in stylish clothes.

Mr. Ferlinghetti was monitor this day. He taught history. He read history. He was history. After he checked your name off the list, he didn't want to know about you unless your name came up in the book he was reading on the Napoleonic Wars.

I went to the window and watched my classmates board the silly yellow bus. Destination Sister School. I sighed, take-me-with-you style. One of those mugs was going to be dancing with *my* girl. Whoever she was.

Metzger came up and leaned on the sill right up against me, also looking out the window.

Maybe he wanted to be friends.

I took the opportunity to try and smooth things over with him.

"This bites, doesn't it? Detention. When we could be heading off right now to meet all those girls and partying all night."

Do people say that? I can't stand words like party as a verb, but I figured the Metzgers of the world did, and if I was going to get along . . .

"Suck my ass, fat boy."

Apparently not.

"You talking to me?" I said. It was either me or Ferlinghetti, right, so he wasn't *necessarily* referring to—

"How the hell'd ya fit yourself into those queer brown jeans that are ten sizes too small? Jam yourself in with a broom handle?"

I told myself he was just making small talk. That Metzger didn't have any friends, so the art of conversation was still a little new to him. I, Elvin Bishop, would remove the thorn from his paw.

"No, I skipped lunch actually, and jogged some too." I smiled. There were about ten guys left to get on the bus, and I told *them* too, in my head, "I skipped lunch. I sweated. I did that, you didn't. I should be the one—"

"I'm gonna kick your fat ass," he said.

Well I tried. You saw. I tried, didn't I?

"Mr. Ferlinghetti," I said. He looked up from his book. He wasn't happy about it. "This guy says he's going to beat me up. Right here."

"You load," Metzger hissed. "You fink. You chicken-shit wimpy sonofa—"

He was right, of course. I had to recover. Just because Frankie wasn't here didn't mean I had to revert to my Mr. Nobody mode. He was putting a lot of work into me, and I could at least show some style. It was safe enough to do anyhow. Controlled, officially supervised circumstances.

"And if he doesn't shut his mouth," I barked, "I'm gonna shove my fat fist right in there." Not exactly how I wanted it to come out, but close enough.

Ferlinghetti looked sleepy, but he had things tightly under control. He looked back down at his book. "Can't do that," he said firmly. Good, good. Just what I was counting on.

I smiled at Metzger. Made him crazy.

"Take it outside," Ferlinghetti said.

There was a loud gulping sound that came out of one of us and filled the room.

Now here's a move I was sure Metzger had never seen before. My knees buckled, I bent at the waist, and with both hands . . .

I grabbed my flaming rump.

Remember what Frankie said about my affliction? About what stress does to compound it? Remember his poor grandmother eating standing over the sink?

"What in the hell is your problem?" Metzger asked, taking a few steps back.

"None of your business," I growled. Then I pointed at the door with my thumb. "Let's go outside."

"Am I supposed to bend way down there to beat your ass?" he asked as he followed me down the stairs. Like he was all put out by the situation.

"'Cause I'll do it. Long's I get to kick your ass somehow."

Every time he mentioned doing stuff to my ass, I winced, and walked a little more sideways.

Finally, as the last party guy climbed on the bus, Metzger and I stood squared off in the school lot. I couldn't believe that Ferlinghetti wasn't even curious enough to come to the window like most teachers would. He even counted on the honor system for Metzger and me to drag ourselves back to incarceration after we were done with each other's asses.

Cripes, the honor system. If I had half a chance, I'd

scratch and bite my way out of this, and at the end of it all, I'd be expected to return honorably to detention?

The bus started up. Metzger started punching air for practice. The dope.

The honor system.

The driver was taking an awfully long time to close that door.

"Come on, Elvin," a call rang out. It was Mikie.

Now there was an idea. How torn should I be over this? How compelled to return to detention? How committed to battling my nemesis with dignity?

How much did I want to meet our sisters?

Metzger bent over to touch his toes. If he was going to make it a game of I-can-do-this, I didn't stand a chance, since I stopped being able to touch my toes at about the age when I stopped wanting to put them in my mouth.

I looked up at the detention window. Ferlinghetti was still tromping across Russia in winter.

"Come on, come on"—this was Frankie. "You gonna waste a killer outfit like that on Ferlinghetti?"

I was weakening.

He started chanting. That is so unfair, the chanting part.

"Sis-ters, sis-ters, sis-ters . . ."

Then, of course, all the bus windows opened at me and everyone in the freshman class—ninety-five percent of whom wouldn't know me if they found me inside their lockers—started egging me on. Like I *had* to go to this thing. Like it would just be no fun without me.

It's the chanting thing, you know. Guys will chant anything, as long as somebody starts the ball rolling. And once chanted, a thing is important and vital and so true you wind up with tears in your eyes you want it so bad. We men are slaves to the chant.

"*Sis-ters, sis-ters, sis-ters* . . ."

I did have this new running skill I'd developed. Shame to waste it . . .

It was so obvious that I was going to cave in to this that the bus driver didn't bother putting it into gear. He'd hauled the door shut with that big robotic arm lever, and now he was going to all the effort of shoving it open again to wait on me.

It was obvious to everyone, that is, except Metzger, who was advancing in a crouched stance, with wide demonic eyes, and the spread-finger lunge of a madman from, like, the silent movies of a thousand years ago.

I was disgusted. "You've never beat up anybody in your life, have you?"

That put him back on his heels. He stopped momentarily, then remembered what he was there to do.

He lurched.

He took a swing.

I took the low road.

"Go, Elvin!" There were chants and hollers from every seat on that yellow bus. The driver started rolling slowly while I motored mightily.

As I stood on the bottom step of the bus, looking

back to blow kisses to Metzger, Ferlinghetti appeared in the window, pointing down at me silently with a mile-long finger.

It is a very good thing that clothes actually do make the man. Because if who we were really depended on what we did, I would have just nullified myself. I'd done the most stouthearted and ballsy thing I'd ever done, running away from detention in full view of the entire screaming freshman class. And simultaneously, I'd done the most snivelly and chickenshit thing I'd ever done, running away from Metzger in full view of the entire screaming freshman class.

And happily, both situations would wait all weekend for resolution on Monday.

So who was I? What was I?

I had great clothes.

"This had better be worth the trouble I'm going to get into, you guys," I said as I sat next to Frank, in front of Mike. The rest of the bus had forgotten who I was already, and moved on to "A Hundred Bottles of Beer on the Wall." "I better be king of the prom here."

Frank squinched up his whole face. "Not smelling like that, you won't be. Whatju do, Elvin, take a bath in ammonia?"

"It's a little sweat, do you mind?"

Mikie put a hand on my shoulder. "Don't worry about him. You're doing fine. That took a lot of guts, blowing off detention. Bring that kind of confidence into the dance with you and you can't miss."

Guts? Confidence? I wasn't aware of having those things before. But now that Mikie mentioned it . . .

Frank would have no part of it. I was like an art project of his, and somebody had spray-painted over his good work. "And your little problem is back, isn't it?" he demanded, taking *my* very personal problem very personally.

"It shows?"

"No, you could have a squirrel down your pants making you walk that way."

"Hey," Mikie snapped. "He's been under a lot of stress. . . ."

Frank put a finger to his lips to shut us up. Then, very quietly, he laid it out for me. "Nobody cares about your stress, so if you want to score, we can't talk about your stress. Got it?"

I got it. I nodded. He really did want something good to happen to me at the end of this, so if I had to take some knocks along the way, well, Frankie was good for me. I was not a baby anymore. I wasn't.

Besides, if I needed to be babied, Mikie would do it.

"He might be right," Mikie said.

Uh-oh.

"So while we're at it, don't talk about your mother. And don't walk sideways. Don't *dance* sideways, for sure. And if anyone does notice your, y'know, difficulty, don't tell them about that, no matter what you do. Instead . . . you hurt yourself lifting weights."

I was trying to be cool. But really now . . .

"With my butt? I was doing butt curls?"

"Lat pull downs," Frank said. "Nobody's going to know the difference . . . unless you keep talking like a jerk."

"So I should stop that then."

"Ya," Mikie said. "I'd say so."

Gotcha.

"I don't see how you can miss, Studley." Franko laughed.

The laugh, obviously, was the troubling part.

BY THE HAND

The dance turned out like tobogganing, where you exhaust yourself dragging the thing halfway up the side of a mountain for an hour, just to spend thirty seconds sliding back down again.

But like tobogganing, you want to do it over as soon as possible.

The first thing that happened when we got into the St. Theresa's auditorium was we split up. The joint was big and cold, a cross between a barn and an airplane hangar with retractable basketball hoops on every wall. I don't know why we split up, I certainly didn't want us to split up, but apparently that's what you're supposed to do. I figured it was some preprogrammed hunting instinct, like when you see the lions on TV spreading out to surround the wildebeest, but as I had always identified more with prey than predator, I was going to have to just play it by ear here. The wildebeest . . . um, prey . . . um, girls . . . were kicking around the shadows of the gym, as far from the entrance as it was possible to get, so we would have to do some serious chasing if it came to that.

The second thing was, the fat kid found me. Nice guy from my homeroom, but friendly enough to make my skin crawl, and I could not commit his name to memory. Apparently because I carried a spare inch or two of midriff, he thought that made us soul mates of some kind.

"Hey, I was wondering if I'd see you here."

All right? Like he's trying to meet *me* instead of snuffle up truffles like the rest of us swine.

"Well, you can stop wondering. Here I am. Bye."

He grabbed my shoulder jokeylike when I tried to slip away. That's another way you can tell how a guy has no friends and no idea. Nobody really grabs anybody jokeylike unless he learned it from TV friendships rather than the flesh-and-bone kind.

"Hey, bud . . ."

And as for calling another guy "bud" . . .

" . . . there's a gaggle of chubby girls. What ya say we go talk to them?"

It'd been a long day already. The Glue Pots or whoever were really wailing over the super-duper St. Theresa's ancient stereo system, and the laser light show was slicing me to bits so I had to lean close to the guy to see how much seriousness was in there.

Tons. Tons and tons of seriousness.

I glowered at him. "Why would I want to do that?"

Jokey shoulder grab with big bear shake. "Ah you clown."

"No, I'm not a clown. I want to know why I'd want to talk to those chubby girls."

Confidence, like Mikie says. Style, like Frankie says. I'm not stupid, I'm not delusional.

But I am not fat. There are people, who happen to have some fat on them, and then there are fat people. This kid was a fat person. I would not be a fat person. Didn't have to be if I didn't want to be. Just don't accept delivery.

"Okay," he said, offended now for god knows what reason. These sensitive fat guys . . . "Because we're chubby guys, that's why. We *match up* with them, okay?"

No. Not okay.

"Oh, like we'll exchange recipes?"

"And because that really pretty one keeps staring at you."

Hello?

"Where?" I gasped. I forgot the entire contents of the previous conversation with . . . the kid. "Where? Which pretty one? How is she staring? Are you sure? Is it something like, this?" I did the Dracula, I vant to suck your blood, penetrating stare. "Or like this one?" I turned a little sideways and fluttered my eyelids coyly like there was a fan blowing hard into my face.

Not that it mattered. The point was that that phrase had never ever wafted my way before, ". . . really pretty one . . . staring at you."

"See for yourself," he said, grabbing the back of my

neck—which was fine by me now—and pointing me right at her.

And you know what? He was right.

There was a whole gaggle of chubby ones.

"Look closer, man," he said, shoving me two inches farther in the right direction.

And he was right again. Her perfectly, impossibly round woman-in-the-moon face was ringed with black curly shiny hair that twisted and snuggled along her jawline, under her chin, along her shoulders, only then to turn back up and reach for her face. It fell over her forehead with the same curlicue determination, like a million tiny silky fingers on a million tiny black hands that wanted nothing more out of life than to just touch the soft pretty surface of her skin.

And I wanted exactly the same thing. Nothing but to lay the tips of my fingers on that soft pretty skin.

And true enough, the startled wide pale eyes were staring right at me. Her eyelashes were long and spiky, top and bottom, like a Venus's-flytrap.

I smiled. I didn't want to, because that was not part of my cool plan.

She smiled back, the rise of her cheek nearly obscuring the lower half of those eyes.

I knew her. Never met her. But I knew her. She knew me. Do you know how that is? How it can be?

What's-his-name didn't have to pull me or push me or talk me into it. Mikie didn't have to convince me, and Frankie didn't have to teach me. I started walking right over to her, even though I couldn't feel my legs and even though this girl in the gaggle was not the plan. I felt my *face* pulling me across the room, to her face, which was hanging there in my sky. I was the tide to the moon of her face.

And my heart felt something. Really, right there in the place where the heart is in cartoons, where Pepe LePew would have this valentine-shaped protrusion punching its way out of his chest. I couldn't believe this stuff actually happened to people in real—

"*Not,*" Frankie barked in my ear as he hit me from the side and moved me like a tackling sled off my route.

"What, what?" I asked, still looking at her.

"No way, Elvin. We didn't come here for that. What has all our work been for? New clothes, new attitude, new Elvin, remember? You"—he poked me in the chest with his finger—"don't belong there"—he pointed at the gaggle, where I could see her peeking out from the black ringlets. She looked confused.

"Why? What? Maybe I . . . maybe. Where would I belong, Frank?"

He spun himself around like a human spin-the-bottle, took in all the action everywhere, then zeroed in on another group.

And a mighty fine group they appeared to be. Not all fashion models and cheerleaders, exactly, but not a bare-knuckle boxing team either.

Now I'm good at being scared. Been scared by pretty much every thing that most people would consider scary and plenty of things most people wouldn't. But this was new. These ladies—pretty and fun-looking and all—scared me cold. That shouldn't have been. Should that have been? Was I doing this wrong?

"They're out of my league, Frank," I said, and nobody would have disagreed.

"Hey, listen to me. You make your own league in this game. Boy, this is your first dance of your first year of high school. You go over there and start grazing with that herd, you might as well just chew your cud for the next four years. For the rest of your *life*, even, is probably what'll happen 'cause this stuff starts right now and goes on forever." By now Frank had me by the shoulders and was trying to shake wisdom into me.

I was paralyzed. This was a lot. On top of a lot. I didn't want to be doomed. Even if I didn't exactly *feel* the stuff he was saying—I kept picturing the curli-cue girl, not the high-style girls—I understood it well enough. He was trying to help me to know what he had always known, but it was kind of like the science guy trying to explain things to the fingerpainting guy.

I was paralyzed, right there in the throbbing gym.

So I did what I do. I turned around to check with Mikie.

But no Mikie.

Like an asthmatic who's lost his inhaler, I started breathing heavily, and pushed off. "Franko, I'll be back. Gotta find . . . I'll be back."

"Don't miss this train, El," he called at my back.

I could imagine the kind of body language he was adding, but I couldn't turn back to see it.

I found him, after weaving in and out of every pod of periphery dwellers. The big brains in the sweater vests, the way-tall guys and way-short guys, the fashion victims and fashion perpetrators, the cross-country track team and the razor-thin air guitar corps.

Mikie was sitting on an overturned milk crate next to the snack table.

"What are you doing?" I asked.

"Watching," he said evenly.

I looked around, then back at him. "Watching what?"

"Watching the world turn. Watching you."

"You're not." Suddenly, knowing that somebody—*this* somebody—might have been paying attention to my movements, made me feel embarassed, like I had done something hideously wrong. I played my actions and nonactions back in my head. What, what?

"Relax," Mikie said with a laugh. "You're doing fine."

It was like I'd opened a great report card. "I am? Am I? What am I doing? I don't know. That's why I'm here. Don't sit here. I need you back there." I pointed out over the dance floor with one hand and gave Mikie the come-with-me wave with the other as I mimed walking toward Frankie and the girls.

"Nah," he said. "I like what I'm doing."

"Which is . . . nothing," I said.

"You know better than that," he said.

And I did. Mikie was never doing nothing. There was

45

always something going on in there, whether I was completely sure what it was or not. Still, I wished . . .

"Come on, Mike. Frankie's zeroing in on a bunch of really pretty girls. You'll like them. There are plenty to talk to. I'm sure there will be one you'll like."

"Ya?" he asked. "Did *you* pick one?"

I paused. Wait now. Right. Why was I here again? Right. "No," I said, half question. "Or yes. See, I saw a girl, and she's not in the group . . . and then Frank pulled me . . . and I suppose it shouldn't matter, right, since I haven't talked to any of them yet, so it doesn't matter who I talk to . . ."

Mikie stared up at me from his milk crate. "You're trying to say something, El."

"Yes, I am."

"What is it?"

"I don't know. That's why I need you. . . ." I did the pointing, waving, come-with-me dance again.

He shook his head. "That's stupid. You don't need me. Go take care of business. I'm going to stay right here and do my thing."

Hmm. "What's your thing again? It looks like hiding."

"Come on, Elvin. What am I doing?"

I thought. I knew. "You're figuring it all out. You're gonna sit there and stare and think and then you're going to stand up and know how the whole thing works, right? Then you're gonna dance and tell jokes and have, like, a steady girlfriend before we leave."

"Ya, that's it," Mike said. "That's what I'll be doing. You caught me. Now will you not worry about how I'm going to do and get yourself out there and meet your girl before somebody else does?"

Confidence.

"You sure you don't want to come?" I sort of pleaded.

He pointed off into the distance. "Somebody's gonna get your girl."

I charged off.

Aimed once again at the girl among the chubby girls. Somehow I felt like that's what Mike had told me to do.

I was derailed once again by Frankie.

"I was just going to say hello," I said.

"Say hello? Say *hello*? Say *good-bye*, goofus, if you're seen with them. Once you get mad cow disease, the foxes won't come anywhere near you."

My nameless friend stepped in. "Do you really have to keep referring to people in animal terms? It degrades us all, men and women."

Frank brushed by him. "Outta my way, Porky."

Frank hauled me right on over to that bright and brilliant and bumpy group.

They were prettier as we got closer.

Louder too.

What were they laughing at?

Shut up. They were laughing *before* they saw me coming.

"That's how you pick 'em, Elvin," Frankie instructed.

"There are plenty of cuties out there, but most of them are about as much fun as tight underwear. What you look for, and what we have here, is the classic laughing group. Fun girls. Good times."

We stopped just outside their loose circle, which opened to a fun and friendly semicircle upon our arrival. Frank took an extra step closer, thankfully taking the lead. He glanced up at the cage-enclosed gym clock, realized the shortness of our time here in this sister-school world, and sprang into action.

"Wanna dance? Wanna dance? Wanna dance? Wanna dance?" he asked each one, pointing a threatening, inviting (a perfect description of his charm, by the way) finger at each as he spoke. No introductions. "Wanna dance? Wanna dance? Wanna dance?"

That about covered it. I would feel like I had to give each girl a box of chocolates just for the privilege of asking for a dance. Frank stared at them like he had already paid them something and was waiting for his change.

"With you?" the leader, the girl Franko, asked.

"Nah . . . well, maybe," he reconsidered after looking at her harder. "Okay. With me."

"Hey," I said quietly, knocking on his back like a door.

"And him," he added.

"No twosies," she said.

"No, no," Frank said, "we're good Catholic boys, none of that. . . ."

Well, they thought *that* was pretty rich. Anyway, it worked, earned me a girl.

"Sure," the boss girl said. "I'm with you"—she poked Frank's flat belly—"and . . . hmmm . . ."

"Me!" one girl called, way too enthusiastically. "I'll dance with the stocky one."

She was something, something special, I had already noticed, because she stood, with the group but not. While the rest were all shoulder to shoulder and pulling on each other's arms to make—I'm assuming—quiet, vicious remarks about fat guys, this one remained untouched, a couple of feet of space around her on all sides, like she was too good for contact.

Not for me, though. She walked right up and grabbed me by the hand.

I must say this thing—first contact, I believe it's called—had a profound, earthshaking effect on me. Cleaned all the old information right off my hard disk. I had a vague notion of another girl I was interested in, of having a home and a mother someplace, but . . .

Franko was so stunned—and jealous, since mine was clearly prettier than his—that at first he didn't even head out on the floor. He just stood there staring at us.

"Should have shopped at the B and T," I said when he finally got out there near me. He continued staring too, while my girl gripped both of my mitts and whirled me all over the gym.

I believe I was doing a bit of staring myself, to tell you the truth. Moving my feet as little as I could, my hips just doing a minor hula thing, and my upper body succumbing to rigor mortis. Meanwhile, inside, I was gyrating unspeakably.

We mingled and muddled about outside while most of the guys reboarded the bus. Me and Frankie and our new gang of sisters (who would, next month, be coming on over to *our* place for a dance). Getting mighty free and easy and chummy.

"We can't wait now," said Frank's dance partner, June. "We'll have a real ball at your dance. Maybe we'll even get started more than ten minutes before the thing's over."

"Ar-ar," Franko laughed, stiff and foreign sounding. Cool, I suppose.

But he was still staring. At my girl Sally. At me. Back to Sally. Up to the sky.

The group of them huddled again, all those girls, and laughed and laughed. It was wild, like one of those 1930s musicals where all the women dress in, like, red sequins and gold glitter and people rip into a song or dive into any handy pool whenever they feel like it. I was expecting to be lifted on a gigantic soap bubble to sing down at the crowd.

Mikie had come over by then, to do what guys do in a situation like this: Glom. He was a ghost all through-out the actual dance, which I knew meant he was de-coding everything. This, then, would be the payoff. I was praying he wouldn't decide to like Sally.

"Hi there," he said.

Hi there? Mikie said Hi there? Did he spend an hour on a milk crate drinking soda and getting his feet stepped on by frosh geeks so he could distill all his wisdom into Hi there?

"Hi there," we all said together.

No girls went rushing to him. He didn't follow up with something clever and winning. He just stood, flat-footed and normal. Just another freshman. He was cool, apparently in a way so ingenious that I couldn't even see it yet.

I may have been focusing too keenly on Mike, because he had to nudge me to look back at Sally, who was looking at me. Right. Back to work.

We were the last, so we did finally have to mount the yellow tube. But not before an almost teary good-bye to the gals we'd leave behind.

"Now, I may not make it back alive," I said grimly to Sally. She played well, squeezing my hands bravely. "But I promise to write faithfully. And to forsake all other girls while we're apart."

"Won't break your back keeping *that* promise, eh, El," my onetime friend Frankie quipped as he stepped onto the bus.

Sally squeezed my hands even tighter. It would have been hurting me by now if she wasn't, you know, a girl and everything. Then she took one of my hands into a sandwich between hers, and rubbed like she was trying to start a fire.

Which she did.

All her friends went, "Ooooooo," then laughed nuttily.

Frankie and I were too cool, the last ones slowly heading up the bus stairs. "I still can't believe it," he said, and we both knew what he was talking about.

"I hear ya," I agreed. "She's not a movie star or anything but . . . she's prettier than *me* by a long way, that's for sure."

"Prettier than *you?*" He was determined that I get the big picture. "Prettier than you? Sure. But man, she's almost as pretty as *me*. . . ." He let it drift off, since that really said it all, don't you think?

When we were sitting in our seats, waving out the window at the girls who were—quite giddily, I must say—waving back, I tried to clue him in. My confidence was pretty high now that I'd successfully completed the day and was safely on the bus where I couldn't fumble it all away. Mike and Frank gave me all the confidence in the first place, so it was only fair I give something back.

"It's the three Cs of success, Frank," I said, clapping him on the shoulder with my nonwaving hand.

You know how weirdly slick and powerful you feel when you are waving and smiling and talking about people who are looking right at you but can't hear? Ya, like that.

"The three Cs. Clothes, charisma, and . . . ah . . ."

I couldn't believe I hadn't thought that through before opening up.

Then, there was the other one. Walking slowly, gliding almost, across the parking lot. The round-faced curlicue girl who knew me already. She turned slightly my way, gave a sweet half smile, which was a sweet half smile more than I deserved.

The false bottom dropped right out from my stomach. My. Oh my my. That's a girl, right there, and Sally was a girl, and they had both paid some attention to me. But that felt so different, what just happened to me. Ouch, it felt different. She walked on.

I turned, a reflex, to Mikie. Like he and she were connected, in my brain. He gave me a fuzzy half smile, and that wasn't right either.

Why, with everything going so right, was everything now feeling so not right?

The bus started moving, creeping. I went back to working on that third C when I noticed the girls, the fancy girls, were doing it to us. You know, the smiling, waving, talking-about-us thing right in front of us but we couldn't hear. I didn't like it one bit.

Then June started waving frantically at Frankie to come out. It was a bit of a mixed message, the way she was flagging the bus down like it was an emergency while she could barely speak, winded from laughter.

Frank booted to the front. The bus driver groaned. "Every time, with these dances, there's always one of ya can't get enough. No public displays, man, or I gotta report ya. You got one minute." And he threw the door open.

I watched—everybody on the bus watched, in fact—as Frank had a brief, intense powwow with June. The chiefs of our respective tribes. Conferring. Consulting.

Cracking up.

They broke, and Franko came bounding back onto the bus. We were rolling again. I had a bad feeling—ah, welcome home, old bad feeling—as Frank came my way staring and grinning. I looked back out the window where Sally was waving broadly and bravely, just like in a war movie.

I turned as Frank deliberately took the seat *across* the aisle from me.

"What?" I asked when he refused to say anything.

"Come on, Frank," Mikie said. "Cough it up. Don't torture the poor guy."

"Okay, Elvin. I think you need to add an extra C."

"Huh?"

"To your list. Clothes, charisma, and creeping crud. Man, all this time you been holding hands with a girl who's got scabies."

Aaaaaaaahhhhhhhh!

That's what I said inside.

This is what I said outside.

Aaaaaaaahhhhhhhh!

Everybody shoved to the back and the front of the bus, sitting five to a bench to stay away from me.

Except my Mike.

SEE ME,
FEEL ME
INFECT ME,
HEAL ME

I kind of thought her hands were too rough and scaly. Damn. Damn. Shoulda listened to myself.

But who knew? How should I know anyway? I mean where's my frame of reference? I just figured girls' hands were supposed to be scaly.

"Yes, Mother, I had a *swell* time at the dance, despite your sabotage."

"Don't say swell to me, Mr. Bishop."

"Okay, I had a . . . smutty time."

"Well, that's a start anyway. Meet any nice girls?"

I shifted in my seat. That hurt. I shifted back the other way.

"So, we're back to that again," she said, pointing at the seat of my chair.

The last thing I wanted at this moment, sitting at the kitchen table in the bosom of my family . . .

"Why do you do that, Elvin? There are only the two of us here, and you're always calling it the bosom of your family. Like it's some kind of misty philosophical dream family you have, and not me."

"Well I *tried* telling people how much I like coming home to the bosom of my mother, but the guys at school started to make . . . remarks."

She thought about that. "I could see where they would, yes."

Anyhoo. I just wanted to chill out, which I could do in my still-sweaty fine duds, with a quick quart of Häagen-Dazs in my lap, and she had to bring up my old affliction, which seems to jump out magically when anybody mentions it, like a lion through a flaming hoop.

A flaming, flaming, vicious red crackling flaming hoop.

"And what's with the gloves?" she pressed.

See, she drinks herbal tea, while I eat ice cream. That's why she's the way she is. How can you reason with such a person?

"I'm cold, okay."

She sipped. "I see. You're cold. That's why you're sitting on one cheek, in wet clothes, with a carton of ice cream in your lap, with my white gloves on."

There aren't a million and a half responses to a question like that.

"You got it, sister," I said.

The sister reference made me flinch. Whole new dimension to that now. Can't call the mother sister anymore. Tough enough to get used to dancing with the sisters.

"I think it's a great idea that you have a sister school," she said.

Just can't let it go, can ya lady.

She waited. I wasn't giving.

"Oh please. Come on, Elvin. Don't make me beg. I can tell by the way you've been slithering around that something happened. It's a girl, right? Isn't it a girl? Oh Lester, he's gotten himself a girl. I can come join you now. I can let go. . . ."

You remember Lester, my dead father?

"Ya, wiseguy?" I said, standing to tower over her ominously. "You think this is funny? You want to go join Lester? I'll give you something to join Lester about."

Ya? So? I hate it when I do this. I can't shock this woman. And even if I do, she'd probably just top me, send me scurrying to my room red-faced, covering my ears and humming "If I Could Talk to the Animals" real loud.

No more. I was a man now. Time for a wake-up call for the old lady.

I pointed a white-gloved finger at her. "She gave me a sexually transmitted venereal disease, how do you like that?"

Where the hell . . . ? I was already humming and covering my ears when I realized the words had come out of *me*.

Right off the chair. I'm not kidding. She fell right off the chair.

"Get back up in the chair, Ma. I want to do that again."

It wasn't a real fall or anything, just something she

does when she wants to express big-time dramatic surprise. When I grew my mustache, she fell on the floor. She couldn't actually *see* the mustache, but she took my word for it and bang she went.

I liked the way that felt. Manly.

The second thing she does, when it really is serious, is she goes to the phone and calls Mikie's mother to see if I'm lying.

See, there she goes now.

"What?" I said, just like I always say. "You don't believe your own son? You have to ask some strangers about me?"

She went on dialing as if I wasn't there. Mikie, the rat, is incapable of lying, and the whole world counts on that.

"What's the big deal, anyway?" I asked, kicking back again with my ice cream, with my dogs right up on the table now.

Sex makes a guy this way. It's all true.

"I *thought* you'd be proud of me," I said, sounding very disappointed in her.

". . . And please, call me as soon as you get in, okay? I'm getting nowhere over here."

"Try Frankie's house now, why don'tcha," I said. Boldness like you read about. Fear, virility, satisfaction, achievement, stabbing rectal pain, all combining to cause wild personality disorder. I was losing it more by the minute. Thrilling, actually.

It was Ma's turn to do some sharp finger-pointing.

"Ya, Frankie. Don't think this whole situation doesn't reek of *that* walking gland."

What I wouldn't give, to be known as the walking gland . . .

The phone rang.

"Now you'll see," I said. "And I want it known that Frankie had nothing to do with this. I contracted my VD all on my own, no help from anybody."

She picked up. "Ya ya. Ya ya ya ya. No! Yes? Oh my god. Disgusting. No, he's proud. Well what else *can* I do? I'm going to boil him, of course."

She glared at me.

Gulp.

She hung up and marched toward me. "That is *not* a venereal disease, Bishop."

"Hey, now, calling me by my last name, now *that's* depersonalizing."

"This is no joke, Elvin. I want you to take this seriously."

"I am taking it seriously. This is a high-prestige disease I got here. I'm the first one in my class to catch something from a girl. Come on, Ma. Let's go out to dinner."

"No. Take off those gloves and show me your hands."

I leaned back in my chair, tossed the ice cream carton onto the table, and tucked my gloved hands up under my armpits. "I see," I said coolly. "Jealous?"

She gritted her teeth, and started counting to ten out loud. But it was all for show. My ma has no temper at all.

"Come on, lady, you can't go on living your life through me. You are going to have to get on with your own existence. You can keep all the framed pictures of me, keep my swing set up in the yard if you need to, play the tapes I made you . . . but really, it's empty-nest time for you, babe. You can't compete with other girls for me anymore. . . ."

"That's it," she said, miming the act of washing her hands, then shaking them to dry. "It's therapy for you, little boy. And I'm not changing my mind this time."

My cool flew right out the window. Even the VD didn't make me braver. It's not that I don't think, maybe, there might be some *stuff* in my head that should be looked at. I just don't want to look at it, thanks. I bolted from the chair, ran up the stairs, and barricaded myself into my room.

Just like every time she mentions the T word. When she finally does decide to get me repaired, they're going to have to send a SWAT team of shrinks to come in and get me out.

"Is she really going to do it?" Mikie asked, very concerned. " 'Cause I'd *pay* to sit in on that." Okay, maybe not *very* concerned.

But I should explain the mystery of Mikie. You may think, What does Mikie get out of this relationship, in exchange for wisdom, understanding, support and all that other ultracool stuff he does for me?

Well, I provide laughs. You have to admit that.

But there's something more. It's like the old "What do you give the person who has everything?"

Needy. I provide needy. Honest, it's like the thing I can do better than anyone, and that Mike can't do at all. So he gets that from me. I can feel it, that when I am in need there is something almost happy that happens to him. And when I'm not . . . well that situation is rare enough that I suspect neither of us knows quite how to act.

So really he doesn't worry when Ma starts talking about shrinking my head. He knows that's where he comes in.

"Every time I start getting manly," I said, "she threatens to call in the mental health authorities."

We were headed for CVS. I had a note in my pocket for some kind of scabies ointment the doctor turned her on to over the phone.

"Does it itch?" Mike asked.

I thought about it. The way you do when you figure you're supposed to be feeling some kind of sensation but you're not, so you try to drum it up. I even scratched the back of my hand a couple of times.

"No, actually. But I'm hoping to soon enough. By the time Monday comes, everybody'll have forgotten my triumph if I don't have the evidence."

"Triumph," he repeated, shaking his head in disbelief. "El, maybe you don't want to keep fighting the therapy idea . . . most people would see scabies as a kind of negative experience."

"Scoff if you will. . . ."

"I will."

We walked a couple blocks silently before he picked it up again.

"Do you know what scabies even are?"

"Of course I do. You're not the only guy in the world who knows anything, Mike. Sheesh."

He waited. The rat always knows when I'm bluffing.

"Ya?" he prompted.

"It's . . . like an allergy. Makes your hands itch. Hives, like."

"*Bugs*, like," he said.

"Get outta town, ya ghoul."

"I'm serious, Elvin. Scabies are disgusting creepy little insects that burrow under your skin and lay eggs there. Then their babies are born—inside you—and the babies dig all kinds of tunnels under there for like weeks and weeks."

I was stopped right there on the sidewalk. My hands were straight out from my sides to keep them away from the healthier parts of me. "Oh my god," I gasped. "It sounded so cute. Scabies. Scabies. Come here, little scabies. Hey wanna pet my scabie?"

"Ya, really cute. And it's the most infectious thing in the world, and it can go on forever spreading from one part of your body to another if you don't get it wiped out properly. Now for the big question."

It took him an hour and a half to ask me the big question.

"Elvin, in the time since you spent time with this girl . . . have your hands been socializing with any other parts of your body?"

I did not dignify that question with a verbal response.

Not for several seconds anyway.

"Oh my god! Nononononononononononononono-noooo! It's so unfair. It's never even been out anyplace. Noooooo!"

"Oh Jesus Elvin don't start that. Crying isn't going to help."

"I am not crying," I insisted as I started jogging, trotting, running, in the direction of CVS.

He caught up. "No? If you're not crying what are those running down your face?"

"*Bugs*, probably," I answered, speeding up.

Mikie caught up quickly, grabbed me and stopped me.

And took my hand.

He grabbed hold of my pus-filled, insect-riddled, corroding hand and pulled me to a stop.

"What are you, nuts? Is this going to be one of those suicide pacts where you want to decay along with me?"

"You don't got scabies, man," he said sadly.

"What? I do so. See, I knew this was going to happen. Everybody's going to wake up and say it was all a dream. No foxy girl held fat Bishop's hand. Well no way—"

"She didn't have scabies. She had psoriasis."

I stared at him dubiously.

"June told Frankie. It was just a joke."

It was just a joke.

It was just a joke.

"It was a sucky joke, Mike."

He sighed. "It was, El."

I went back to walking. "What part did you like best?" I asked, steaming. "The part where I thought the girl liked me? Was that the best part, Mike? Or was it the part where I was ready to peel my own skin off when I realized what I had?"

I did not remember ever scolding Mike before, ever. It was weird, like I was getting angry at a part of myself—like I was one of those people who injure themselves on purpose.

"Never mind," I said. "Forget it anyway."

"Well," he said, "no, we shouldn't probably. You might, y'know, maybe have a point."

No, really, I did not want this. I was so off-balance, hearing Mike stumble and apologize. I'd rather be wrong. I'd rather have him back the way he was. I *needed* him back the way he usually was.

Oh. Just like he needed me?

"She really did like you, El," he said, reading my thoughts for the hundred millionth time. "The joke was bad, but I think really, she did like you anyway. You were doing great at the dance. Better than I ever would have thought . . ." His voice trailed down and away there.

"And we don't need to go to CVS anymore," I said, staring at the CVS dead ahead.

"Yes we do," he said, looking me up and down as we walked.

Which caused me to look myself up and down as we walked. I was now traveling with a nearly completely sideways gait. Like a football drill where the coach makes everybody follow his hand like dummies, left right back left right, cut this way, cut back.

I was once a football player, have I mentioned that?

"Your problem is out of control, friend," Mike correctly said. "I think as long as we came this far, we should really get you fixed up. Can't stand to see you like this, man."

I punched him hard on the arm. As long as I was facing that way. "Well, *you* didn't help it any. Scaring me with all that scabies bug crap, when you knew I didn't even have it—"

"Cut it out already, El. I feel bad about that."

"Ya? Well not bad enough. So now I'm like, full, like I got a complete grapevine growing out of my ass. I am redefining Fruit of the Loom. Maybe I could get a sponsorship deal . . . stop laughing at me . . . so, no, feeling bad is not good enough."

"I know it's not good enough. But CVS must have something for, er, people like you."

And there we were. People like me. I didn't just have a condition now, I had joined a community. Frankie was right. These things really did happen only to certain kinds of people. And it was looking more and more like I was simply one of them.

I was fourteen years old, and I figured by now I had experienced everything there is, except, of course, the one or two really big ones, but what was to come at CVS was a trip I'd never figured on taking.

"So, how do we do this?" I asked as we walked tentatively into the superstore of medicine and hygiene. We at least knew enough to keep moving. Perpetual motion is the way not to look suspicious when you feel guilty for not doing anything. Once you stop and stare, the security cameras all train on you, the shoplifting beepers start screeching, the Simon and Garfunkel tape stops humming over the PA, interrupted by the manager's voice bellowing your name over and over for everybody to hear, and the girl behind the counter starts dialing up your mother.

They think you're looking for condoms.

I went right to browsing the endless magazine and paperback aisle. They had about two million titles, divided into categories. Women's magazines, men's magazines, teen, fashion, sports . . . paperback best-sellers, romance, John Grisham.

"Everything in the store falls into a category," Mike said. "There's a category for you too. We just have to find it."

I stopped flipping through *Travel & Leisure*. "Well sure, let's just look for the Ass aisle."

"Or you could ask someone."

I tossed the magazine in disgust. "I will *not*. Gimme

a break here, will you? I'm embarrassed enough that *you* even know. I'm not asking any stranger for help."

"Then do your funny walk around the store a couple of times and let them figure it out for themselves. They are professionals. They'll get it."

See that? That is the problem. Mike was just playing, and in fact I wished I had said that line. But instead of laughing, I just got worse. It was stupid, really, and entirely my own fault, but I could not get past this. These people had seen it all, and probably nobody cared what my problem was any more than they cared about the lady with the wart on her finger or the guy with the tickly cough. So it shouldn't have mattered.

But of course it did. This was just one of life's little jokes, a problem that for no good reason is funnier than other problems. And I like a joke as much as the next person—*more* than the next person, unless the next person is my mother—but there is a large difference between making a joke and being one.

I walked up and down and up and down the aisles without picking up one item that might help relieve my distress. I couldn't even bring myself to give it an honest effort. I grabbed a tin of Band-Aids from aisle five, which would hardly be the best solution; a box of Kleenex from six, for all the crying I'd likely do if I didn't get real help; some cold medicine; and a shower cap.

All the time, I must have been doing The Walk. Because as I stood reading all the ingredients in Tylenol Flu Formula, a large red-faced obese man in a baseball cap and farmer jeans crept up on me with a sad smile and a familiar ridiculous sidestep.

I was afraid. I stood frozen.

"Aisle one, friend," was all the kind stranger said before padding away.

My god, there it was. My community.

Mikie, you ask? My good and lifelong friend? Trailing behind me, keeping just enough distance to allow me to maneuver in relative privacy, but close enough to rush in and help if I got in over my head with the hemorrhoid crowd.

But things got serious when we went to dark and mysterious aisle one. There was no fun in aisle one. Sad faces, puffy faces. I was the only shopper in the region without a hat. We all pretended we were there for something else—sure, grab some Pepto, or have yourself a plantar wart foot pad shaped like a tiny life preserver—but those things were decoys. We knew why we were there.

I wished they wouldn't make eye contact.

When I finally reached my destination, there were three packages that seemed to address my problem. Two of them actually had the words "Burning" and "Itching" written in acid red there on the cover, which I thought was nice of them.

Some time must have passed, because Mike came up and tried to hurry me through this. "Preparation H, right?" he said, snagging a tube. "Take this. This is the stuff."

"Duh!" I said. "Of course I know what it is, I live in

America, after all." I looked at the package and growled at it, rather irrationally, I suppose. "Even the *product* is too embarrassed to come out and say its own name. Like we're going to think it's for headaches, or heartburn, or hair loss, and those things are all okay."

Mike tried to bring me back. "So try it, El. It's on TV, so it must be the best one."

"'Fast, temporary relief,'" I whisper-barked, imitating the guy on the commercial. "I'll say! It was so fast and temporary I didn't even get the cap screwed back on before—"

"All right, all right," he said, waving me down. "We'll look for something else."

Quickly, speed-reading like a brainiac, I whipped through the product descriptions and instructions on the back of another box. I shoved another into Mikie's hands for him to do the same. It would have gone a lot quicker if the two of us hadn't kept looking over our shoulders as if it was the nudie magazines we were sweating and panting over.

A big hand fell on my shoulder.

"What is it, boys?" the manager asked me.

"Huh? Huh?" I asked, startled. "What is what?"

"The deal. What is the deal? I noticed you been prowling our aisles for an awfully long time. Now fun is fun, but we get enough prank shoppers in this store—"

"We're not pranks, sir," Mikie said.

"Good. So then why don't you tell me what you need, and I can help you on your way."

"I don't need anything," Mikie said happily. "I'm with him."

Mike and I must have looked like one of those old married couples I always saw bickering over medical stuff in drugstores. "See that?" I snapped at Mikie, forgetting the store guy completely for a minute. "It's so bad *you're* embarrassed, and it's not even your problem."

"Okay then, what is it you need?" the man interrupted. He was very tall, that manager. "What are you sweating about, son?"

"I . . . ah . . . I, it's a condition. I have a condition."

There, I said it, right? Whew, that wasn't so hard.

"Well then, you're in the right place. That's our business. What do you need to help your condition? We only want to help you."

Come on, Bishop! I screamed internally. It's Stand and Deliver time. You are a man now. You messed around with a woman, for crying out loud. Messed around with her hands, anyway. You got VD, sort of. You shop at Big and Tall—you can handle this situation.

It's natural. Nothing at all to be ashamed of. This guy sees it every day. Well, he probably doesn't *see* it every day. . . .

Tell him!

The manager sighed. "You want condoms, don't you, kid."

Oh my god. Stress. Stress.

That was it—something had to be done. It was time to act.

I dropped my basket and ran like a rabbit. Like a sidewinder rabbit.

Mikie followed right at my heels.

"Well, that was an excellent decision," he said when we were far enough away from the store that I could stop running. "Now you don't have your cure, *and* CVS is off limits. Pretty chicken there, El."

"Ya, well if you were any kind of friend you'd have stayed there and bought the stuff for me."

He paused long, but for effect, not because he really needed to think about it.

"Nobody's *that* kind of friend, Bishop."

Bishop. He was calling me Bishop now. The great beast was distancing me from everybody. . . .

"Anyway," I said, "it's not really an issue anymore, because I think . . . ya, I think it's going away now." I smiled bravely. I winced. "Ya, there it goes."

I smiled. I winced.

Damned if Monday didn't eventually come around. I did feel a little better before that. Didn't get scabies. Or psoriasis or VD or malaria for that matter. And there were no new eruptions on any other parts of my body since I avoided all stress by spending Sunday reading magazines and watching a *Ren and Stimpy* marathon.

But then, Monday.

"Now, where were we?" Metzger asked. I swear, he spent the whole weekend frozen in the spot where I'd left him on Friday. Same location in the school lot, same grimace on his face, same sumo squat. Looked like he was the one with the 'rhoids.

"Where were we?" I shot back. "Well you obviously were right here. I was everyplace else."

"There's no way out this time. I'm gonna kill you now, chickenshit," he said. He was very angry, apparently. He was also right. I couldn't run away this time because I had to go to school.

Guys were filing past Metz and on into the school as if he wasn't there, even though he was making a pretty good spectacle. This was quite a thing, since most of these guys would stop dead and watch if it looked like a pair of *beetles* might start fighting on the sidewalk, but Metzger just couldn't generate that kind of interest.

So I figured, me too.

I stared straight into his eyes, angled toward him with my fists clenched and my teeth clenched. He stiffened, readied.

And I walked right on past and up the stairs.

Caught the boy pretty well flat-footed, I reckon.

"Hey," he shouted. I'm sure he could have done better if I'd given him more time.

"What?" I said. "I whipped your butt on Friday, why should I waste my time again?"

"You . . . the hell . . ."

I left him tripping over himself. Why not, right? Who's to say I didn't, you know, in the big picture, whip his butt?

I was handling my bully issue pretty well, don't you think? Now if only all my other issues were as stupid as Metzger.

At lunch in the cafeteria that day, Mike, Frank, and I were visited by a major senior personage. One of the biggest and toppest of the seniors—one of the elite whose boots Frank'd been licking on his way up the social ladder—came over and hovered above our humble table. His name, spoken only in hushed tones around here, was Darth. And yes, he's as warm and fuzzy as it sounds. But not in any obvious way, not like your regular teenage bully. This guy, if we were in an old movie from the 1930s or something, would be smoking a cigarette in an ivory holder. And he'd have a little pencil-line mustache. Girls and their mothers would love him. Nice shoes, quiet, smooth manner. But there is a big-time scariness in there that is kind of like a dog whistle, recognizable only by dogs—meaning guys.

Yet, at the same time, he was—there's no other way to say it—irresistible. He didn't speak directly to just anybody, but it was exciting when he did. You got a sense in every conversation with Darth that you were going to get shot to smithereens the next time you sat in a barber chair. But it almost didn't matter. Like it would be an honor to get creamed by such a guy.

Such a guy.

He came up behind me so I wasn't even aware until I saw all the other ground squirrels like myself scurrying away, and the table became covered in a darkness like a solar eclipse.

"Hey, Darth, man," Frank slurped. "Have a seat. Can I go stand in line for you? They got the spice cake today. Can I get you a spice cake?"

Since Frank didn't have the dignity to be embarrassed for himself, Mike and I blushed for him. The three of us, and Darth, were the only ones left at the table.

"Ya, do that. Go get me a spice cake."

Frank was gone like a rocket. Darth turned to Mikie. "Go help him get me a spice cake, would ya?"

Mike is no lapdog. But he's also no punching bag. So when he just sat there in the face of a direct order from Darth, at least I had the good sense to sweat like a pig. Frankie stood frozen halfway to the cake line.

It was a quiet, tense, damp moment, which did not seem to have a solution. Until one just happened.

Darth nodded at Mike. Like an agreement. It was amazing to me, but really it shouldn't have been. See, if I had tried to do what Mikie did, I'd be wearing my underwear up over my shoulders about now. But this is Mikie's thing, how he always makes his way, and people just seem to get it, to go with it. And for Darth, well a lesser criminal probably would have tried to break Mikie, but instead he seemed to appreciate him.

Which is not to say Darth doesn't still get what Darth wants.

"If you wouldn't mind, Michael," Darth said, sounding very reasonable.

Mikie nodded back at him, and got up.

Leaving me alone with Darth. A newsworthy event. I'd have never expected it. The other freshmen and sophomore lowlifes—whose eyes peeped and blinked in our direction like raccoons from the Dumpster at night— certainly never would have put this scene together. I figured trembling was probably the right thing to do.

"Quit the shaking shit, will ya?"

Okay, wrong. I froze.

Darth nodded at me and gave me a friendly smile. I returned same.

"Nobody, and I mean nobody, ever woulda believed it." He said it like this was the continuation of a talk we'd been having for weeks even though our one previous exchange had consisted of this:

"You gonna finish that?" He was referring to my lunch. It was not lunchtime, we were not in the cafeteria, I had not *started* the lunch, never mind finishing it. In fact, I had been walking into the building at the beginning of another fine school day, swinging my brown-bag lunch at my side.

I had stopped, stared at the bag, and nearly wept, knowing what was in there. Two Underwood chicken spread sandwiches on oatmeal bread, the oil of one of them making a glorious clear stain on the side of the bag like the pioneers' windows that were made of paper that they would then smear with—

"I said are you finished with that?" He was an impatient businessman when you didn't keep up with him.

75

"Sorry," I had said, handing over the bag. "I was day-dreaming. Just checking, but, it would be futile to resist, right?"

He'd looked concerned for me. "Yes. And possibly dangerous."

So, really, this would be our first chat, but it felt like we'd known each other for a long time.

"When we heard, me and the guys were all sayin' that if we were going to bet on something like this, you would have been probably the second or third last—maybe the fourth if you lost a few pounds—but anyway close to the last guy we ever would've figured."

It seemed that needing to know what he was talking about was not as important as going with the flow. I shrugged. "Me too. Goes to show you never can tell, huh?"

"You never can."

He leaned close, put a fatherly arm around my shoulders. "So hats off to you, guy. Who gave you the VD?"

Ah-ha.

Well this was certainly a type of popularity I never figured into the bargain.

"You know!"

He laughed. A most insulting laugh, actually. "Of course I know. I'm *me*."

"Wow," I said, and meant it. "That's kind of shock-ing, that you can know everything, about everybody. And so quick. Like the FBI."

"Whoa," he said modestly. "Not everything, of course. I don't know, like, what your grades are, or when your birthday is, 'cause I don't give a shit. And I wouldn't know if, say, a guy got sweat socks in the mail from his grandma for his birthday. . . ."

My god. Did it mean he controlled the U.S. Postal Service, or my gran?

"But VD? You don't get VD around here without me knowing about it. That's like, my thing."

Such a lovely thing. And now it had brought me and Darth together.

"VD killed George Washington," Darth shared. "And Al Capone. Did you know that?"

There you go. Another fine community I'd gotten myself into.

"I didn't. Thanks."

"But you don't want to die."

"Uh-uh," I agreed. "Not today, anyway."

Darth scanned the crowd in all directions, looking for authority figures who outranked him, like maybe the Pope. Then he pulled a little something out of his sock. Under the table he slipped it into my hand.

It was a tube, like toothpaste only smaller, more metallic, stiffer and colder. I brought it up to the table-top to get a better look, but he slapped my hand so I lowered it again.

I squinted, craned my neck, stretched, stretched. Must have looked like I was eating lunch out of my own lap.

I giggled with a thought. From my position there with my face in my groin, I shared the thought with my new friend. "Hey, if I knew I could do this I never would have gotten myself into trouble in the first place."

He slapped the back of my head. I jocked myself with my own chin. Another first.

Finally I could read it.

EXTREME UNCTION.

I popped my head up, not knowing what to say. I took a shot. "Cool."

"It is, it's very cool. Minty, even. Like Vicks VapoRub, only better. And very special rare stuff. Imported. Not available elsewhere."

"Great. So what's it for?"

"It's for your problem."

"My . . . ?"

"Your pecker problem."

"Ah, yes. Of course. What then, a teaspoonful a day?"

He slapped me on the back, laughing. "You're funny. We gotta keep you alive for a while, I think."

"That'd be good."

"Ya, so what you do is, whenever Mr. Fizzy starts feeling like he's gonna fall right off—and believe me, you're gonna feel like you wanna let him—you just slather some of this stuff on it, and the fire will go out. Clears up some o' the crust too."

Crust? Oi.

I spoke more softly now. Not to be more secretive, but kind of like when one guy gets kicked below the belt and the whole group talks funny for a while in sympathy. "This is the cure, then?"

"Nah. It's better, though. The doc'll give ya pills to cure it. This'll just make ya *feel* good through the rough times. Some o' the guys put this stuff on even when they don't got anything wrong with 'em, that's how good it is."

Wheels turned.

"So it's not, you know, disease-specific? It's more of a general . . . salve?"

"Ya, that's it. Salve-ation, right?"

"And I could put it on, say, a cut, or . . . a rash, or something . . ."

"You mean your 'rhoids? Sure."

Is *nothing* sacred?

I curled back up into snail position. "Thanks. 'Preciate it. See ya 'round."

He smirked. A smirk of disbelief. Showed me his big hairy palm. Yes, hair growing in the palm. "And it's only gonna cost ya two things," he said way kindly, which was way scary.

"Only two?"

"Yup. The first is fifty dollars."

"F—? Darth, I don't have fifty—" I stared down at the tube of EXTREME UNCTION. There was nothing written on the label other than the name. And *that* looked like it was hand-lettered.

"You can't get this in any stores," he said, sounding like a Ginsu salesman on TV.

He was gently waving both hands now to ease my

fears (which was of course *fanning* my fears). He'd gone from brotherly to fatherly to grandfatherly in short order. I was sinking fast.

"You don't have to pay me right now. It's your good fortune that I also finance."

Does it sound to you as if "No, thank you anyway, Darth" was an option? Nah, me neither.

"Thank you, Darth," I said as weakly as possible.

"And the second thing is even simpler," he said brightly. "All you need to do is give us your solemn-oath confirmation that this girl—her name is Sally, if I'm not mistaken—did in fact give you this problem."

Oh. Oh my. That was the *simple* part then? A quick calculation left me with the options of either lying and dragging another person through the mud with me, or—gasp—disappointing Darth.

Now, while our friendship was still kind of new, it did trouble me greatly to think of disappointing him.

And who was "us"? How did Darth become multiple all of a sudden?

What to say?

My disease had made me popular. I'd get a badly needed reputation, one I'd never be able to actually earn on my own. And I'd get to keep my lunches. Anyway, maybe I didn't have to lie. How did he put it? Did Sally in fact give me the problem? Well, sure, the whole thing with the hands. Scabies, VD, psoriasis, what's the difference, really?

Just one bit of clarification, and I could get through

this. "Now, solemn oath means exactly what here?"

Darth sighed. Breaking me in was wearying him. "You will find, Elvin, that in dealing with me, you are playing on the field of honor. Honor is all that matters. Trust. I trust people not to let me down. When you do that, people tend to *not* let you down. The honor system is the best system."

Ah, that again. I've worked with that system before.

"Yes," I said. "Sally gave me my problem."

By the time the words had left me, my stomach was doing flips, my mouth had gone dry. It had seemed, when Darth presented it, so simple. And then, it was so not.

Darth stood up. "Enjoy the ointment," he said, walking away from me as if I had a disease or something.

Does it seem to you that I just did something bad?

GREASING THE SKIDS

I felt better just holding it in my hand.

The ointment, ya pervert.

It was like a magical thing, like inside this small, obscenely expensive tube, was the gel that controlled my popularity. Everybody wanted a piece of me now.

"I cannot believe," Frank said, "that after all this time with my nose up that guy's ass . . ."

Is it just because I was oversensitive to the issue at this point, or did people generally make ass references way too often?

". . . he turns around and buddies up with *you*."

"Do you have to say it like that?"

"What? Say what?"

"*You*. The way you said *you*, meaning *me*, was like I was something stuck on the tip of your finger."

"Sorry." He seemed to mean it. "Can I be your friend?"

Sigh. "You've been my friend for a long time, Frank."

"Ya, but now I want to *tell* people."

This time the sigh was out loud, and unintentional. "Sure, Franko, you can tell people. Why did I think popularity was going to be more fun than this? Why does it look so good on you? Is it like a suit, or a nice fabric like silk or something, that it just hangs better on one person than it does on another?"

Then, after a pause, Frankie sighed back at me. Which was something. He doesn't pause before speaking, as a rule. And he does not sigh publicly. "Okay, El, listen to me. This is what I want you to do. Ready? Don't pay attention to what popularity looks like on me. In fact, don't pay too much notice to what I look like at all."

"What are you talking about? I thought you were showing me how great it was to be like you?"

"That was before Darth. Okay? Darth is, like, not a nice guy, you know?"

"I don't know," I said, the old nerves acting up as we got too near to serious. "He has a certain—"

"El," Frank snapped. "Popularity can be expensive."

He wasn't talking about the fifty-dollar unction. I was this close to joking my way right out of this conversation. If I had not known how much Frankie had endured to make his way into the inner circle, I would have.

"Okay," I said. "Thanks, I got it."

We were heading out the door at the end of that long and trying day, when I was stopped. Another one of my new fans.

"Hi there Mr. Ferlinghetti," I said queasily.

"Well good afternoon, Elvin," he said. He was acting all cool, like this was just a casual accidental meeting even though he had himself planted in front of the main exit, and he was without a book.

"See ya, friend," Frankie said. "Can't help you with this one."

Ferlinghetti led me silently up the stairs into the detention room, where there were four other detainees already there policing themselves.

"Go on, get out," he said to them as we walked in.

They sat there, stunned.

"I mean it," he said. "You're free to go. Emancipation Day, 1863. Go on before I change my mind."

Say this for the boring old crock: He was never at a loss for a mind-numbing historical reference to suit any occasion and send 'em heading for the aisles.

"Now you," he said to the only "you" in the room, me. And he said it just like Frankie had.

"How many million days of detention are you going to give me, Mr. Ferlinghetti?"

"None. You've already sentenced yourself. Cowardice is its own hell."

So was this. It's a hard word, isn't it? Cowardice. Made me flinch when he said it. Made me retreat.

"Me? Oh I see. You think I was running away from a fight there on Friday. But that wasn't it at all. I wasn't running *from* a fight, I was running *toward* love. And it paid off. Guess what happened to me later on? Go on, guess."

84

He stared down at me like one great carved stone leader of many armies, many nations. A figure so sure of himself in his bravery and wisdom and true-blueness as to be the complete inverse of myself. He didn't even care about my big news.

"A coward dies a thousand deaths," he thundered, in a voice that would bring god to his knees. He pointed me toward the door.

There was no retreat from it this time, though. The word, the *concept* seemed to have my name embedded in it. And it couldn't really have all that much to do with Metzger, could it?

I was off my balance here, off my game. I could handle an exchange like this normally, but something was wrong.

"That's it?" I asked. What did I want? I was getting off easy. Wasn't getting off easy a *good* thing? Wasn't it, in fact, the focus of my life until recently?

Yes, until recently.

I needed a real, tangible punishment for fleeing, one that would clear my conscience and let me get on with my simple little existence. "Come on, Mr. Ferlinghetti, is that really it?"

"A thousand deaths isn't enough for you, son?"

"No, I mean, I can go? You're finished with me? There will be no further punishment for running out like I did?" There should be, if you ask me.

He stared hard at me, growled, then got all revved up for one last blow.

"Be a man. A coward dies a thou—"

"I'm going, I'm going," I said, scurrying for the door before he shook out the beams and the building collapsed and left me with only 999.

But really, the only thing I was escaping was the building.

"*You've* gotten awfully popular all of a sudden," Ma said when I finally came in after school. "You've gotten a whole slew of phone calls this afternoon."

"Me? A whole slew? How many's a slew?"

"Two. But one of them was a *girl*." She giggled the word "girl." Like this was some kind of big deal. As if I didn't get calls from girls all the time.

"A *girl*?" I gasped. Back off, Elvin, back off. Be cool. "I mean, oh, a girl. That's nice. Who else called?"

"Somebody named Metzger."

I wondered how long a thousand deaths take.

"And the girl's name?"

"Sally."

"Really? That's the girl from the dance." I fingered my tube in my pocket. "Did she leave her number?"

Ma started frowning. About the VD thing, I figured. "I didn't realize it was *that* girl. She didn't sound diseased over the phone."

"Mother?"

"Don't call me *Mother*."

"Fine. Medusa?" I asked. "Did Sally leave her number?"

"Why don't you call Metzger back first. He seemed more anxious to talk to you anyway."

"I bet he did. Where's the number, Ma?"

She tipped me off, letting her eyes drift over to the note stuck to the refrigerator. I made a dash for it.

She made a dash for it. We got to the refrigerator at the same time. We both seized the note, and a mighty struggle ensued.

"Give it up, lady," I said, trying to peel her fingers open. She had the note in her fist.

"You'll thank me for this, Elvin. She's no good for you."

"I know she is," I panted. "That's exactly what I'm after. Gimme the number."

"Call Janey," she grunted, holding tight. "She'll go to the movies with you."

"Janey's my cousin, Ma."

"So what? That stuff doesn't matter till later."

I broke away, gave up, threw in the towel. My eighty-year-old mother was stronger than me.

"I'm thirty-five, Elvin, and very wiry. You have nothing to be ashamed of."

Once we had established that she was tougher than me, and could manhandle my life however she wanted to, she handed me the paper.

I dialed. Waited. Three rings. Just like the circus, I thought. "Hello? Is Sally there please?"

I must admit, on the phone I am everybody's dream date. Nice manners, melodious tone . . . and the guilt

I was feeling probably gave me just the right hint of bad-dog whimper.

"This is Sally."

Angelic herself. Her voice made my blood sugar rise—made me feel all was right with the world. We could get through this. We could get past any bad thing I might have done. She probably didn't even know what I said about her, so maybe I could make her like me enough before it got back to her. . . .

"This is Elvin Bish—"

"You swine!" The yelp was so piercing it shot straight through my left ear all the way to my right, giving me two simultaneous earaches. "You worm. You deluded, doughy little mushroom."

She had heard. And now I would hear. How could I have thought . . .

No, she was right, I was a deluded mushroom.

I paused to let her breathing get slower, and less audible, while mine got louder. Then I began at the natural starting point. "I'm sorry."

"Why are you doing this to me? I have gotten six phone calls just today. All seniors from your school. They all want me to go out with them."

Oh boy. Who'd have thought . . . something *I* said would have so much weight. "You hear from a guy named Darth?"

"What? No. Not today, anyway. He's called me before but . . . no, he's a *cool* guy. I'm going to get calls from all the *other* kinds now, thanks to you. You probably scared all the Darths away, ya rat."

I had a small moment of relief over this. There seemed to be a bright side. "Well, maybe that's not so bad, broadening your—"

"Every one of them wants to make a date for six to eight weeks from now."

I was way out of this conversation, and falling fast. "That's not right. You shouldn't have to commit so far in ad—"

"And I'm gonna kill you for it!"

"Hey, that's enough now. I'm on my mother's phone, for godsake."

She started hollering into my mother's phone. To make an indelible audio impression that would still be echoing later when Ma picked it up. "You should buy your son clothes in *his* size, Mrs. Bishop!"

"I'll hang up," I threatened.

"Try it," Sally dared.

I tried. Got the phone one inch away from my ear. Couldn't do it.

This was a *girl* I had here on the line, for cripes sake.

"I'm really pissed, Bishop."

There seemed nothing else to do but retreat into my comfy delusions. Reality was too hard.

"Hey, did I get this mad when you gave me VD?"

"I DID NOT GIVE YOU VD!!!"

I sighed. Details, details.

"Oh, well, not exactly. But you did give me a sexually transmitted dis—"

"I did *not*."

"Well, scabies, you gave me—"

"Not! Not! It was a joke, you moron."

I paused now with the memory. Oh yes. The joke. What was *I* apologizing for?

"Oh, right, the joke, me moron. Well guess what? Now you have psoriasis *and* a reputation. I guess we're both pretty funny people, huh Sally?"

The screaming resumed.

Click.

I did it.

What the hell. As long as I was on a roll, Metzger's phone number was right here on the same slip of paper. Why not call up and chew the fat with ol' Metz. Or maybe I'd call him 'Ger. Probably, he wants to arrange a little cease-fire. A meeting of the minds.

"Here's what I'm gonna do to you," he said. There followed a goose-pimple-raising screechy noise, louder than Sally, but not as loud as a train smushing an abandoned car.

"Was that a cat?" I asked calmly.

"And I *like* him," he said as a response.

"I want to help you, Metzger," I said. Phones always made me brave. No thousand deaths for me as long as I could phone my life in. "Can I call you 'Ger?"

"Screw."

"Okay then. So listen, I think talking to me just makes you crazier. So I'm gonna give you another number that'll help you mellow out. It'll cost you three bucks for the first three minutes and fifty cents for each additional minute, but you'll feel a lot better. Tell 'em I sent ya. Just mention my name, and I betcha they moan."

"Oh, you're gonna moan, all right."

"Except for 'moan,' I don't believe you heard a word I said."

"Cut the jokes, all right, Bishop? Everybody's laughing at you enough already. You can't just run away forever, you know. I'm gonna catch you eventually, and then you gotta do something. So why don'tcha just cut the crap and be a man for once, grow the hell up, huh, Bishop, ya wimp? Ya fat loser? Everybody knows what you are, you know. And everybody's laughin'. But they ain't laughin' at what you think."

Well then.

Mr. Metzger surprised us all, didn't he? Did what nobody expected.

He shut my mouth. That short speech had to count for at least two deaths right there.

"You know what shithead Ferlinghetti said to me?"

I really wanted to believe that Ferlinghetti didn't talk to Metzger. You know, like he gave me the talk because he saw something more in me, something salvageable.

"He said it's better to die on your feet than to live on your knees."

There's that death thing again. How come Metzger's talk only included one and mine was a thousand?

"What were you doing on your knees, Metz?"

"Keep laughing, funny boy . . ." he said.

Click.

This time it wasn't me. And I wasn't laughing.

EXTREME UNCTION.

I was lying on my bed in my underwear, looking at the label.

EXTREME UNCTION.

What the hell is unction anyway? One might say it would be the intelligent thing to find out before I slathered an extreme dose of it on any of my favorite and most necessary parts.

Dictionary says it's an act of anointing. Well, I suppose, if we want to make an official ceremony out of this . . .

Or something soothing and comforting.

There we go. EXTREME comforting and soothing? That's for me. Bring on the unction.

I disrobed completely. Was lying there, exposed. Tube in hand. Looking at the tube. Looking at the ceiling. Looking at the tube. Looking out the window. A bird flew past the window and I quickly pulled the comforter over me. Started again. The tube. The window.

The door opened.

"Jesus, Ma, you could knock!" I pulled the spread up to my tearing eyes.

"I'm sorry," she gasped, slamming the door shut immediately.

That wasn't good for either of us.

"I'm sorry," she pleaded again outside my door. "I'm sorry, I'm sorry. I'll go now. I'll leave you alone."

"Thank you," I said, relaxing slightly.

Until I realized what she thought.

"I wasn't doing that!" I yelled as she padded back down the stairs.

"No, certainly you weren't," she said. "Just . . . forget I was there, and go on about your business."

"Ma! Ma! I wasn't doing that."

Downstairs, I heard her pick up the phone.

"Oh, my, god," I said, scrambling up and into my thick white terry-cloth robe. I flew down the stairs.

She was already at it. Nodding, nodding to the other person.

"I didn't," I insisted.

She smiled sweetly and nodded. She put her hand over the receiver and spoke to me, "Go fix yourself a snack—you're probably hungry now."

"I'm not hungry, and I don't . . . do that."

She patted my cheek. "I do the laundry, Elvin, remember?"

I went and got a snack.

She pulled away from the receiver again and said to me as I popped a couple of Vienna sausages from the can, "See, they say it's perfectly natural. You have nothing to be ashamed of."

Cripes. The Sons without Fathers helpline. That's how she spends *her* three dollars per minute and fifty cents for each additional . . .

Every time they tell her to tell me I have nothing to be ashamed of, it humiliates me like mad.

NOBODY'S FOOL

"You think I'm a fool, Franko?"

"Cripes, El, is this what this is all about? You gotta prove something?" Frankie asked as he led me shivering down the stairs to the basement level of the school. Into the inner sanctum of cool-guy territory, Darth headquarters. "Sure, you're a fool, but you're an awesome fool. You're great at it."

I followed him down, down. Didn't say anything. I thought about what he'd said and didn't disagree with it. He was not trying to hurt me. Fool was my thing, my gift. It didn't just happen to me; I cultivated it.

In other words, it was my own fault.

"Well what if I don't feel like being that anymore? I mean, what if lately I find myself feeling, like, embarrassed to be me. I should change that, don't you think?"

At the foot of the concrete steps, he turned around to face me. "Ya . . . well . . . ya, fair enough. But is this really where you have to start? You know, nobody just *gives back* something to Darth. Especially if he's expecting to be paid for it."

"Right," I said, maybe being a tad optimistic, but hey. "But he'll have to understand. I didn't use the UNCTION at all. My condition is getting better on its own. I never asked for any ointment, he just forced it on me."

"Well," Frankie said, "that's kinda what he does."

"Well, I never asked for it, didn't need it, and don't have that kind of money to pay for it. So I'd have to be a jerk to take it." I puffed myself up and breathed deeply before making my big statement. "And I have made a decision not to be a jerk anymore. Starting here."

He shook his head and led me farther on. "El, buddy, you do make your own life as difficult as you can possibly make it."

"I live for challenge. For danger and intrigue." I still had a little jerk left in me, obviously. But a little might get me through.

"Well, boy, you found it this time," Frankie said as we stood in front of the throne room of the Dark Kingdom of Christian Brothers Academy. "I don't know what intrigue is, exactly, but I do know what danger is, and it's right in here." He pointed at the black metal door, with the ominous words stenciled on it in white.

PHOTOGRAPHY CLUB
DO NOT OPEN DOOR IF RED LIGHT IS ON.

The red light was on.

"It's not too late, Elvin," Frankie said. "You can

change your mind. Not for nothin', but *I* don't want ya to do it. Maybe we can get the money. I'll do, like, a kissing booth or something. . . ."

I shook my head. "Don't worry about it. I don't think he'll even be thinking about the money, once I tell him that I lied about Sally."

Frankie just grabbed me by the shoulders and shook. We didn't even attempt to have the obvious discussion about the latest of my thousand deaths. Just the grabbing and the shaking.

I pointed grimly at the red light.

"Sally will get over it, Elvin. That's just nuts, man. You're risking—"

"Not much." I held up a hand like I was trying to answer a question in class. "How often am I serious, Frank?"

He gave it a moment of thought. "Not a lot."

"Right. So at this moment, about this thing, I am really serious. And you can see that it's, y'know, important."

Frank continued to stare at me. Took a breath like to argue, then nodded. He rapped out a bizarre series of beats on the door. The light went out. We went in.

"Yo, Frankie," somebody said. I recognized that somebody as the number two knucklehead, Obie.

"The *Photography Club*, Yo-Frankie?" I asked. "You and your wicked hombres hang out in the Photography Club?"

He whispered desperately to me. "Shut up, El, or I'll have to hit ya."

"You'll have to what?"

"I'm not supposed to let anybody wise off to me without smacking him. That even means you, and I don't want to have to do that, or even know if I'll be able to. And I also don't want to find out what happens if I'm supposed to hit ya and I can't do it. It's the code thing. So if you talk to me in front of them like you usually—"

He was still whispering in my ear when I yelled out, "No, Frankie, for the last time, I will *not* touch you there, I don't care if you do have a pack of Rolos in your pocket!"

My, did we get some looks from the gang.

My, did I get a clap across the back of the head.

"That's gonna cost you," I said.

He shrugged. "Sorry, El. You did make it easier than I thought it would be though."

"Ah," Darth interrupted, "you two done with your little spat? Or would you like us to clear out so you can have some privacy?"

The rest of The Boys laughed hard at that, as they did at all the right places when The Boss spoke. Odie, Okie, and Obie, whom we bottom-feeders knew affectionately as the Psych-Os. This group was all too familiar from the boot camp the school ran for incoming freshmen, Twenty-One Nights with the Knights. Alaska doesn't have nights as long as each of those twenty-one nights was, but Frankie claimed it was the greatest experience of his life. Made a man out of him. It's entirely possible that I just don't know what a man really is, but the truth was these guys broke Frank there. In ways that I could see but mostly ways I couldn't, they humiliated him and tortured him and made him crawl before making him one of the chosen. It was a weird thing, and scary to me, that he had to hit bottom to get to the top. But he does have some kind of power here now. I guess that's what he wanted even if he seems equal parts scared and happy.

"*Now* look what you did," Frank said. "You know what he's saying, don't you? Huh?"

He seemed pretty worried about it.

"Gee, Frankie, I don't. Does he mean that you and I really do quarrel too much, and it's, like, messing with the special *energy* of the room?"

"Keep it up, wise guy. You know what they're already calling you, right? The Velveteen Sphincter, because of the hemorrhoids, how do you like that?"

"The Vel—" I actually laughed. But it was the old laugh, the kind I did only because I couldn't think of what else to do. The jerk laugh.

"That's coldhearted," I said.

"Thanks," Darth replied. He put an arm around my shoulder and led me over to the photo-developing table. Everybody gathered around like it was a board meeting.

I was still reeling over the nickname thing. "I don't see how I can even enjoy the book anymore now, *The Velveteen Rabbit* . . . I mean you really changed the meaning a lot."

99

"See?" Darth said, laughing and pulling me harder around the neck. "I told you guys, didn't I? I told you he was more of a funny than a dink."

I tried to turn my head to look at him, but it was pretty well locked. It occurred to me, feeling that grip, that this was serious. Darth thinking I was funny was not just good for my social life. It was looking rather important to my physical life as well. I rolled him my eyes. "Thanks," I said.

"So, what are you here for?" Obie snarled. Obie didn't like me as much as Darth did. And he didn't like the fact that Darth liked me, so it was likely to get worse. Also, Obie, two-way football star and local juvenile-delinquent-about-town, was known to be a steroid connoisseur. His eyes came across the table at me two feet in front of the rest of his skull.

"Okay," I said, realizing that all the fun and hijinks was pretty much over.

"Answer the question for chrissakes," Obie snapped.

"Lighten up, man," Frankie said, sounding like a six-year-old version of himself. At least he made the effort.

Obie wrinkled him with a stare, then returned to the business of withering me.

"Okay. I came because I have to tell you something."

Okie leaned across the table. Okie, like his bookend Odie, was the less scary brand of football meathead, the big doughy offensive lineman type who would be an athlete for exactly four years, but who would then graduate high school, marry his first cousin, twice, put on another sixty pounds, lose all his hair, go to work for his father-in-law uncle at the auto parts store where he could sit on a stool that fit his rump like a yarmulke and tell people all day we'll have to special order that part for ya buddy. I kind of liked him.

"Is that it?" Okie asked. "That's what you had to tell us?"

"I wish," I said.

Darth released his grip on me, gave me a gentle-enough push away from him to look me over. "No," he said sagely.

"No," I said.

"He has something *more* to tell us." Darth could see. That's why he was the brains of this outfit.

Frankie nodded.

"You can go now," Darth said to him without looking at him.

Um, um, um, ah, um . . .

"Oh," Frankie said, likewise surprised. "Well, I thought I'd stay, you know, help out—"

"And *I* thought you'd go," Darth said very seriously. This time he did look at Frank head-on.

And he was gone. I started doing this ridiculous little hyperventilation thing as I saw him leave, and only then realized how much I needed him. How much his hard-earned cool was swaddling *me*. Before walking out, Frank turned to me and shrugged, winked, and gave me a thumbs-up.

Shrug-wink-thumb. The triple! Oh my god, I was a dead man.

"Speak," Odie said.

Badgering the prisoners was apparently his one Photography Club function. But he did do it very well.

With the creepy low light of the darkroom, the closing-in feeling of the group, the silent isolation of our location at the far end of the school bowels, the situation reminded me of a World War II movie when—

"What *is* that?" Obie barked again. He was pointing to me and talking like I wasn't there. "You ask him a question, and he takes like a century to answer." He leaned up close to me, started poking me in the forehead with his badly unclipped index fingernail. "What're you *doin'* in there?"

Wouldn't you like to know, peckerhead? I mentally taunted him. Thumbing my nose, flipping him the bird, mooning him, all the things I'd have done if I were an actual tough guy. I was just about to—

"No, really," Darth cut in. "We haven't got all day." He looked at his watch. "And if this is somethin' we gotta beat you for, y'know that's gonna take us twice as long, so we need to get on with this."

"Of course," I said, sensing my opportunity. "The fact is, I came to tell you some really good news." I reached into my pocket and slapped the unused fifty-dollar tube of EXTREME UNCTION on the table. "It seems I won't be needing this," I said, boldly. "You know, since I've begun a new lifestyle, taking better care of myself, I'm feeling a lot better. So, if you don't mind, I'd like to return the merchandise."

It's amazing how high some people can raise one eyebrow. Darth's looked like he'd swept it back over his hairline. "You don't say? The VD just kinda went away, did it?"

"Oh." Almost forgot about that. "Well yes, in a manner of speaking. I was gonna get to that—"

"Well, how about your other little problem, then?"

I'd nearly stopped experiencing the other little problem, that's how good the situation had gotten. However, in the heat of the moment . . .

I squirmed in my chair.

"Fine as wine." I smiled bravely.

"Crushed the grapes then, didja?"

I shifted back the other way.

"Well, no, it's a combination of proper diet, moderate exercise, and avoidance of—"

"I say we check and see for ourselves," Obie said, without even a suggestion of impish humor. Obie had a certain future as a foul one-of-a-kind criminal genius.

Thank god the *sane* evil bastard was the one in charge.

"Strip him," Darth commanded, folding his arms across his chest. "I'll prepare the photographic equipment."

The four of them got busy like worker ants, moving chairs around, testing conditions with a light meter for just the right look, bending me over.

I contributed a quiet gentle sobbing.

"No," Frankie said, bursting in through the door.

"Hey," Okie screamed. "The light was on out there. Darth, he came in and the light was on. No knockin' or nothin'."

Darth shook his head but smiled too.

"This ain't good for you, Frank," Obie said. They'd pretty well forgotten about me now.

"You don't really need to do anything to him, right?" Frank asked.

A loud, satisfied sigh came out of Darth. "You passed," he said to Frank.

"Huh?"

"Ya," Obie said. "Huh?"

Darth elaborated. "We need this. Loyalty. This is good. You can't teach that to a guy. He came in here to rescue his pudgy little friend . . ."

Hey! I thought. I'm not . . . Ah, save it for later.

". . . even though he could wind up very sore for this. I'm impressed."

Frank allowed himself a modest smile. "Thanks, Darth man."

"Shut up. Get in the chair," Darth answered. "Velvet, you can go."

Holy smokes. I didn't want this. I didn't want the other thing either . . . but I didn't want this.

"I'll stay . . . with my friend . . . thanks," I said, acting as if he had offered to freshen my drink rather than to get the hell out.

"Get the hell out," he clarified.

With that, the two linemen grabbed me by the arms and showed me the door. "I thought you were impressed with the loyalty thing," I said as they stuffed me out.

"Who gives a shit if *you're* loyal? You ain't a member," Odie cracked, giving me a kick in the pants as a good-bye.

But they couldn't make me stay away from the door. I hung tight to listen in case I needed to barge in heroically, but it was a pretty thick door. I could only catch snatches of conversation.

" . . . *your* mistake, Frankie . . ."

" . . . can't just let this go . . ."

" . . . maybe gotta decide . . . if you're a sphincter . . ."

What am I, a *species* now? All my friends are sphincters?

" . . . or are you cool?"

There was a long pause. Long, long, long. Those are the worst. Nothing ever really happens when people are talking, does it? It's always in those pauses. I began to sweat. There were a lot of these pauses at the summer camp, and after every one Frankie came back a little bit less Frankie. I was there to clean him up at the end of it, but cleaning a guy up isn't the same as helping him out, is it? A little late is too late, that's what I thought then, and it was what I thought now. Frankie was in there because he wasn't going to let it happen to me.

Then, chairs shifted. Then there was banging around, scuffling, grunting.

I was almost ready. So, so scared. Almost ready. Don't make me come in there. Please, god, don't make me.

Louder grunting. Something big tipped over. But it didn't sound like a beating so much as they were all working together to rearrange the furniture.

Still, I should . . . I should have been in there . . .

But he came out.

Glistening. His face had such a high sheen, especially around the nose and mouth, even I could not sweat that much in that short a time. Only I guess I had. Drenched, I was. Probably shining just as brightly.

But he didn't look destroyed.

I didn't care how oily we looked.

He didn't say anything. He walked right past me, and I fell in line behind him. Down the corridor, up the concrete steps, holding the oak handrail of the ancient wrought-iron bannister for support. Across the checker-board of two-foot-square green-and-white tiles in the school's front lobby, and out into the street, where we leaned for home.

"I was just about to come in there, y'know, Frankie," I said. "I swear, I had my hand on the doorknob. I was all set to knock, wait for the light . . ."

He waved me off. Not like a go-to-hell wave, which might have been appropriate, but a forget-about-it wave, which was unbelievably cool of him.

"Well . . . thanks, anyway, you know . . ."

The wave again.

I felt terrible, wishing there was some little something I could do.

Well there was, wasn't there? I could tell him.

"You're . . . you're really a man, Franko. I mean, like, even more than you think you are."

He stopped, turned to me, and shook his head. He drew a deep breath and swallowed, as if speaking was hard for him.

"Don't worry about it," he honked.

"What?" I hardly recognized his sound. And the shine of his face was . . . oh no . . .

"Don't worry about it," he repeated, without any help from his sinuses. He sounded something like a deaf person trying to speak for the first time.

I could see now. The inside of his nose was clogged solid, with clear gel.

I pulled out my hanky. I never use it. I never even take it with me, but somehow it's always there in my pocket when I need it. Don't know how she does it.

I watched somberly as Frank blew a pound of EXTREME UNCTION into my hankerchief.

I couldn't wait till my mother came across *that* mystery in the laundry.

He handed me the mess, and we walked on.

"Thanks, Franko. You saved my ass and—"

"Your *fat* ass," he corrected.

". . . saved my fat ass, and saved me fifty bucks to boot."

He shook his head.

"What?" I nearly cried it. "What? What now? Don't these guys have anything better to do with all their talent than to—"

Frank handed me the expelled, flattened, chewed(?) tube of UNCTION. Then he handed me a new, full one.

"No, no, no," I wailed.

"No cash refunds," Frank explained. "Merchandise exchange only. And, since they concluded that the original tube had been opened and used—"

"No!"

"And that you were now coincidentally cured . . ."

Oooh, oooh. Oh, how *wrong* they were.

"And that you can never be too sure about these things, that you could have another flare-up at any time, what with the stresses of everyday life . . ."

"Frankie, where am I gonna get a hundred bucks?"

"No, no, no. You're a bulk buyer now, and they really do like you. So it's only forty."

"Still a rip-off."

Frank gave me a big-brotherly pat on the shoulder. "You won't think so after you see the way it can also clear your sinuses and soothe that nagging tongue-ache."

"And I never even got to tell them the other thing, about Sally . . ." I started—really—back toward the Photography Club. Frank made no attempt to follow. I stopped short, his caution a fairly sobering chill. I turned to face him. "Timing, I suppose, would be important here."

"I only got two nostrils, El. Let's not force them to get creative."

He's very good at saving me, Frank is. I ran to catch up as he headed out.

ALL THE WRONG PLACES

"I've been thinking about your situation," Ma said, taking me on a frighteningly chummy walk to the garage.

"Which situation is that?" I asked, staring at her hand draped over my shoulder.

"You know, your loneliness problem. Your isolation, your weirdness."

"Ma? I am not weird. Why would you say something like that?"

"So, I got you something."

I couldn't believe it had deteriorated so badly that she'd talk right through me. Time to turn up my volume.

"You got me a *car*? Ma, you're the balls."

"I am *not*, thank you very much."

I ran ahead to yank up the garage door. "I can't believe you did this. I cannot believe you were soooo cool. . . . Oh, this'll fix everything. No more loneliness, no more isolation and weirdness. You were right, Ma. . . ."

I struggled with the massive, heavy, rusted green garage door that opened upward, floor to ceiling. I squatted like a power lifter and heaved, but still only got it up about a foot.

She came up to help me. "Elvin you are fourteen years old. I did not get you a car. How irresponsible do you think I am?"

"I don't know," I said, letting go of the door when I realized there was no five-liter Mustang on the other side. "You let me get *this* bad, I figured maybe you'd let me be screwed up *and* happy."

"Well," she grunted, "I won't."

Finally, she got the thing up enough for us to slide under, while I stood there tapping my foot and saying, "I'm waiting."

Though, in reality, I could have waited some more.

"You're joking," I said.

"No," she squealed, all excited about what she'd done. "Come here, boy," she said to it. "Come on. Come meet Elvin."

"We've met. And he ain't coming."

So she went to him.

"He's just a little worn out from all the excitement," she said, picking up the little bundle of joy and cradling him like a camel-hair dog-faced baby.

She meant well. She really did. And mostly I liked her. She didn't slap me around or bring home bald fat men who smelled like second-day souvlaki on a stick and called me "sport," and she was there every day when I woke up and she fed me and laughed at my old *Monty Python* tapes even when nobody else knew what was

███

going on. She bought me Mr. Bubble and then poured it into a Head & Shoulders bottle so that my friends wouldn't see when they were prowling around the bathroom looking for clues. She was all frigging right.

"Ma, ya big goof," I said. "Do you know what you bought?"

She played simple to keep me off balance. "A basset hound, I believe."

"Wrong. You bought a throw pillow. And why? What were you thinking?"

"I was thinking, mister grateful, that it would be nice if you had a puppy. A boy should have a puppy, and I realized you never had one. No puppy, no siblings, no father . . ."

She misted.

Hell.

Damn.

See, we don't do this. Me and Ma, we have a nice tidy deal. She doesn't mist on me and I don't mist on her. There are better ways.

I chose to ignore it.

"So what did you do, Ma, did you, like, *advertise*, for the lamest, neediest, most useless lifeless beast in captivity?"

"Hell no," she said. "Look what happened last time I did that."

"What? What last . . . ?"

Oh. I get it. Good one, Ma. She's back.

"Actually, I needed help deciding, so I took Mikie

with me. And he told me that you've had your eye on this little guy for a long time."

Oh, now *there* was a move. Chalk one up for Mikie. Genius. Mikie the dead genius.

Ma was getting more attached to the thing every second. Squeezing him harder and harder, to no effect. The dog just kept molding himself to whatever shape necessary, parts of him collapsing, parts of him squeezing between her fingers like a water balloon. I got closer and patted him. He felt like a knot of laundry hot from the dryer.

"I just figured, El, you've been kind of mopey and lonely . . ."

"Oh, I get it," I said, stepping back. "This is from when you caught me in my room, isn't it! Ma, you thought I was . . . jeez . . . which I wasn't—so you bought me a *dog*? First, I wasn't doing what you thought I—"

"It's all right, it's all right."

She shut her eyes tight when she said it.

"They had a monkey. It was a cute little squirrelly thing. But it kept doing . . . well, doing what *you* were doing, so I figured *that* was no solution."

It was okay to rant at this point, don't you think?

"But a dead basset hound, that's a solution, Ma? Oh, wait a minute. I think you're right. I think it's working. I think I'm cured. Let's go watch *Baywatch* and see if I need to run to the bathroom and jiggle the handle."

"Elvin!" Ma gasped.

That's the move. Shock the old lady into submission.

"He is *not* dead!"

So much for the provocation.

"The man in Puppy Palace said he'd probably be a little shocky for a few days . . ."

"Shocky? Well sure. The world's changed a lot since he went in that front window. There were still four Beatles last time this dog saw the sun . . ."

"He is going to be fine, Elvin Bishop."

Ah, the full religious flowering of my name. Sure sign the discussion is over.

"I got him for a very good price, and it included a ten-pound bag of—"

"Methadone?"

Ma and dog walked away from me then—well, Ma walked, dog draped—toward the house. I could see, by the hunch of her shoulders, by the scuffing of her feet, but most of all by the complete absence of anything like a joke, that I had done what I hadn't meant to do. What I never meant to do. Not to my ma.

What to do, what to do? Like I said, emotional territory, not where we Bishops tread.

I caught up to them in the driveway. I wrestled him away from her, the two of us tugging on legs, scruff of neck, various and ample folds of excess dog. Dog appeared not to notice.

I won. I pulled him close, then draped him around my shoulders like a fox stole. "See," I said, "a very useful dog."

She started walking away.

I pulled her by the arm.

"I love him, Ma."

She stared at me.

"*Love*. Him. I love him so much. And I don't even know what I would do without him."

She smiled. I smiled. She went to the house. I went to the garage.

Dog went back to sleep.

LOVE MITES IN THE AIR— PART ONE

But you know what? In her round-the-twist way, Ma was right. Dog started helping me out with my relationship thing. Thanks to him, I saw her again. The girl.

The girl. The curlicue girl with the shining black hair, the round face, the eyelashes like two small Japanese fans waving out at the world, cooling the world just that little bit.

Except she made me warmer.

"Hi," I said, and it was a struggle, coming out like ten or twelve syllables. I was standing there with Dog, in front of the Ark veterinary clinic where I was taking him to have his narcolepsy checked. She was coming out of the Indian restaurant next door, eating some yellow meat on a stick. "That looks good," I said.

"Do I know you?" she asked, tilting her head like people do when they want you to know that they are not really puzzled at all but are, in fact, pretending to be for show. Only I didn't care if she was faking or really confused or what, but when she tilted her head and closed one eye—*boom*, was the sound of that one eye closing—well all I could do was stand there trying to think up ways I could go on puzzling her so she'd look like that over and over again.

"This is my dog," I said, holding Dog out like an offering of food. I realized I still had no name for him. Not that he deserved one. But people expect . . . "Grog," I blurted. Pretty accurate, I thought, for a spur-of-the-moment christening.

"That's a very nice name." She didn't really seem to think so. "But I asked," she repeated, "do I know you?"

"Oh, yes, well sort of. We almost met at the dance last month. You were looking at me, and I was walking over to talk to you . . . come on, you remember. . . ."

She tilted her head back in the other direction, closed the other eye—*boom*. It may have been that I had genuinely puzzled her this time, but it was all the same *boom* to me.

"Sure you remember. I was with a chunky guy. We were walking over to you . . . you were with a bunch of . . . other girls. But before I got there, my buddy bumped me. . . ."

"Are you the guy with the scabies?" She pointed at me, aha style.

"No, I don't have any—"

"Yes, now I remember. You're the guy who gave scabies to poor Sally."

"Now *that* is untrue. I can't believe . . . no, that story has to stop."

The girl waved at me and walked away, as if I had finished. I didn't believe I had, though, so I pursued her. I put Grog down on the sidewalk. "Come on, Grog, come on," I said, trotting on, until the leash tightened. I turned, and of course he was lying on the sidewalk like a basset-skin rug. I scooped him up and ran.

"No," I insisted, catching up to the girl and walking alongside her. "Sally didn't even *have* scabies, she had psoriasis."

She shook her head. "Well, I don't see how you could have given her that."

"I didn't. She gave *me*, that is, neither of us gave—"

"Did you catch it from him?" she asked, motioning toward Grog then quickly withdrawing her hand.

"What? Psoriasis? Dogs don't get—"

"Scabies. Lots of times I hear people pick it up from their dogs. Is that why the two of you have to see the vet?"

Oh, she was good.

"I told you," I said, "I don't have scabies, and neither does he. He just doesn't move, that's his problem."

She finished her yellow meat, offered the stick to Grog. To my surprise, he took it, but then just let it hang out of the corner of his droopy kisser like a movie detective with a cigarette.

Then she picked up the pace, as if the stick had been slowing her down. I struggled to keep up, carrying fifty thousand lifeless pounds of narcoleptic dog.

"Can you tell me your name, even?" I asked as she

opened up a sizable lead on me.

She turned to face me while continuing to reverse out of my reach, out of my life. "Why am I of such interest now? It has been a month."

Yikes. Do the questions continue to get harder?

"Or is it that your VD has finally cleared up so you're back in circulation?"

Yup, the questions get harder.

Because she was right. See, you can know something for a minute, and then not know it again because . . . well because stuff gets in your line of vision. Or because stuff gets out of your line of vision. In this case, at that dance Franko bumped me off the beam. Sally got into my line of vision and this girl got out at the same time. Sally was lots of great things. She was beauty for sure and she was popularity, and she was all those things I thought were not that important to me but I suppose actually were. And then there was Frank buzzing in my ear and me the jerk totally unprepared for any of this and so.

So this one got bumped out and stayed out a whole month and I see her again and I'm thinking jerk again. Me, not her. Although it's a very risky thing to do, sometimes Elvin needs to listen to Elvin. And I was telling myself the first time I saw this person, Yup. I said that. Yup. Yup. Yup. I knew it that time and now I was knowing it again and I could be sentenced to an outcast social group or to Devil's Island but if this girl would change her mind and pay me some attention I would be lucky enough and happier than a jerk has a right to be.

"Hello?" she asked. "What is that, like a trance thing you do? You and the dog, you had like the exact same expression."

"That was all a misunderstanding, all that stuff about . . ." Then it occured to me, and I got one more cheap little thrill out of the situation. "So, are they saying that about me, over at St. Theresa's?"

She turned once more and hurried off down the street.

Jerk, I said to myself. *This person would not be impressed by VD!*

A little yip, sounded like a yup, came out of Grog. First sound I ever heard him make. Pretty sad little sound.

And then I made it too.

I forgot all about the appointment with the vet. Walked straight on home and then not only did I not do anything further to correct his behavior—or, his *lack* of behavior—I reinforced it by joining him.

"What is with the two of you?" Ma asked as she walked into the living room and found dog and boy both spread wide on the carpet the way sky divers look right after they deplane.

"We're tired," I said, convincingly, I think.

"How'd it go at the vet's?" she asked, crouching down to stroke Grog and look into his one open eye. "Did they give you pills for him or something?"

"Ah," I hemmed, "we didn't exactly go to the vet's."

"Why not?"

"'Cause I think he's better. Y'know, we got all the way there, we were standing right in front of the place, about to walk in, and I swear, he made a sound. So I figure he's cured, and we could save the twenty bucks."

Now Ma looked at me very suspiciously. She left Grog and walked over to me on her knees. She stooped way down low, leaning on her elbows. Then she took her thumb and gently pulled one of my eyelids way open to scope my brain.

I braced myself for the joke. She had to. That's what I would have done if I were her. But nothing like that came. First she pulled away from me, got to her feet. She stood, stared down in my direction, and smiled. No wiseguy smile at all. Almost an apologetic look, and surely unsure.

What she saw inside me she had never seen before.

No dope, my ma.

LOVE MITES—

PART TWO

Don't bother ever planning anything to go the way you want it to. That's all I want to say.

I figured I slept for about a hundred hours. Fell asleep there on the rug, and barely remembered getting rousted by Ma and staggering to my bed. Grog, no slouch at the sleeping game himself, put up very little fight when she hauled him back to the garage.

"Ma!" I called when I woke up feeling mighty. She wasn't around, and I needed to show mighty to somebody. I stood in the doorway of the kitchen, hands on hips, waiting. Then the back door opened. Calmly, arms folded, lips curled in a friendly snarl, Ma appeared before me. I took a deep breath to start again.

"Ma!" I announced. "Ma! I feel like this is going to be a big day for me. I can feel it, something's going to *happen* today."

Her smile broadened. "Something already has. Come with me," she said, backing through the doorway the way she came, then leading me through the kitchen, out the back door, down the driveway to Grog's apartment.

I heard a small chuckle bubble up from deep in her throat just before she heaved up the garage door.

"Oh my god," I yelled, "Do something. Those rats are killing Grog. I *knew* we shouldn't leave him in the garage."

I looked away. Ma grabbed my face and pointed it back at the scene.

"Jeez, he is so stupid!" I screamed. "Do something, Grog! Defend yourself!" I turned to my mother. "He doesn't even know he's being attacked. When do you suppose it'll register?"

"Elvin?" Ma asked, prodding me.

"What?" I said. "They are rats."

"Elvin? You're in denial."

I have superior denial skills. Watch.

"I am *not*," I said. So much for that.

"El, what's the big deal? It's a pleasant surprise, that's all—"

"Mother," I snapped. "After a lot of years of confusion, I finally figure I've got all the gears grinding the right way . . . then this." I gestured with an open palm toward Grog the miracle dog and his children. "You're telling me now he's had babies? Now what, I have to start over and try to figure the whole gender thing all over again?"

"We made a mistake," she said calmly.

"Did we now?" My turn to be sarcastic.

She giggled as she spoke. "Well, Elvin, they *told* me it was a male. . . ."

"They lied, I think."

"Who could tell, with all the folds and the hair and everything. . . ."

"You bought me a pregnant dog."

"Not really . . . they gave it to me. I *wanted* to buy you the monkey."

I stared hard at Grog. In amazement. In anger. This was too much. Not now. Not now. This was supposed to be *my* day, the day I changed everything, the day *I* started socializing in a big way. I really didn't want to know about this right now.

"No," I said.

"It's a tad late to just say no, Elvin."

"How could this be? Wouldn't he have to . . . you know . . . *move*, to get this way?"

Ma covered up her mouth with her hand. She was laughing hard now. "That's not the best part," she said. "Go have a look up close."

"I don't wanna," I said.

"Go on."

Slowly I approached. I crept, I crept. I got close, tapped one of the offspring on the shoulder. It stopped dining to look over its shoulder at me.

"Oh my god!" I squealed, jumping up, jumping back, bouncing off a trash barrel and scurrying back behind my mother. "Ma, did you *see* that?"

She nodded, covering her lower face now with both hands. "Horrific, no?"

* * *

I could thank Grog for one thing. He gave me something to be distracted about while I sweated the approach of the single most important event of my life. The dance that would change me irrevocably, that if I botched I would not have any reason to ever leave the house again . . .

You see, I needed the distraction.

For a while neither of us could speak. I did a little shallow, noisy breathing, some stretching exercises, and a good deal of perspiring. Mike did nothing lifelike. I knew what was wrong with me. But I did not know what was wrong with Mike, because nothing was ever wrong with Mike. He was, as we neared kickoff, slipping into dance weirdness mode, just like the last time.

Fortunately I knew what we both needed. To talk about something else.

I tried to describe the situation to Mikie as we sat stiffly in the stands of our gym, waiting for our sisters to arrive so we could dance with them.

"What do you mean he had babies?" Mike asked. "Elvin, that's impossible. And I'm very surprised your mother hasn't had this conversation with you yet. Y'know, she leaves all the hard stuff for *me* to do . . ."

"I know how it works. Apparently, Grog is not a boy dog."

"You've had him for almost a month, El. Y'know, you could have checked by now."

"It's not my fault," I protested. "He's got all that hair, the loose skin, the folds . . . even his ears sweep the floor, on the rare occasions when he walks."

Mikie nodded sympathetically. "He did come with a lot of extra material, huh?"

"I knew he was a girl all the time," Frankie said from his spot flat out on the bench. He was lying there, stretched out, facing the ceiling but with eyes closed, hands folded across his chest. He was concentrating. Frankie treated dances and parties the way starting pitchers treated the opening game of the World Series.

"Right," Mike said. "How did *you* know?"

"Because I'm Frankie," he said, and it didn't even sound like a boast, just like information, like info from the phone company. "If he's a female, I just know it, that's all."

"Ya," Mike popped, "and if he's female, odds are you've dated him."

Frank sprung up in his seat, the way dogs do when they hear something nobody else can. "That's cold," he said with a smile, carefully smoothing out the front of his shirt, then standing to do the same with the razor-sharp crease of his pants.

"And you guys should *see* how ugly these creatures are." I added. "You can't even tell what kind of animals they're supposed to be."

"See," Frank said, starting his descent down out of the stands just seconds before the door opened and the girls filed in, "I'm cleared. If I really was Grog's boyfriend, those would be damn handsome puppies."

With Frankie and his bizarre yet enviable pride to

lead the way, the entire freshman class walked down out of the stands, and stopped. We stood, in one fine, motionless row at the foot of the stands, on our side of the gym, across from *them*, the girls, lined up identically over on their side, as if we were all here for nothing more than a boys vs. girls game of Red Rover Red Rover.

Only this time was different. This time, we were experienced. We knew how short an hour could be when you were trying to meet some girls.

And, they weren't *girls* anymore. They were *a* girl, and a bunch of other persons. A very different thing really. Scarier, even. Sweeter. Scarier.

"Cripes, Elvin, what *are* you doing?" Frankie wasn't waiting for anybody, and when he started into their territory, I was close behind—because he had me by the shirtfront. Followed by a lot of second- and third-tier dancing fools.

"Yo!" Brother Cletus called before we'd gotten three quarters of the way across. Brother Cletus was the guy who was assigned to manage these things. We figured he was the most qualified because he had moussed-up hair and wore one of those gold Italian fertility horn pendants on a chain on the outside of his black holy-business shirt.

He was pointing at Frankie. "I'm watching you, Frankie. Keep that in mind. I'm going to be watching you."

"Okay Brother, watch me," Frankie said politely, without slowing down. Then he whispered back to me,

"He's gonna go blind watching me."

Frank went straight to June, and was already on the dance floor before anybody else even started with their chat-up lines. Then I was there standing in his wake, having sort of blindly followed along behind him, into June's circle of friends, where I was face-to-face with Sally.

Was this what I'd intended? This wasn't what I'd intended. Wait a minute. What was I intending?

"Did you do the right thing?" Sally said, grim look on her face.

Holy smokes. Holy, holy . . .

"Course he did," Frankie said from a few feet away. Dancing, listening, talking to June for himself, talking to Sally for me. Taking no chances. Working all the levers.

"You did the right thing?" She was not convinced, but she was willing to be. Her face brightened a bit.

The right thing. The right thing? Did I even *know* what the right thing was? I could almost hear the snappling in my head, like a frayed electrical wire.

"Elvin Bishop," Sally said, snapping her fingers in front of my face.

"Elvin," Frank called, making the *get on with it* rolling gesture with his hands.

Voices. Music. Stuff. Ugly puppies. That buzzy feeling in my belly. There was a point. Where was it? Did something bad. Wanted to do something good.

"She got a friend for me?" came the voice of the

individual glommed like a mussel to my stern. It was the fat kid.

I wanted to be kind. I am kind. I used to be fat. I used to be kind.

It used to be simpler.

"I told you. Nobody's got a friend for you."

"Ya," he said, "but you got lots of girls. Couldn't you introduce me to one?"

Lots of girls?

I was looking straight at Sally, who was looking up at the ceiling. I was thinking about . . . who, now? Somebody else. Confused, I was here now. . . . Sally . . . Sally is very pretty, isn't she. . . . Sally, who was now tapping her foot, checking her watch, whistling—the fully mimed version of time passing.

And passing it was. Frank had by now circled around behind me, placed his hands on my hips, and was guiding me toward Sally. "Ya, it was hard, but Elvin's a stand-up guy in the end. He did the right thing, Sally, and your rep is back in order."

She smiled. Not, like, joy, or love or anything. Just, okay, good enough. So she tugged me out of the harbor and into the deep water. Mid dance floor.

I was at first just happy to be there. Found myself mostly just watching, as Sally danced in front of me, dancing, yes, like girls dance. Which is to say, dancing well. Her weight shifted from one foot to the other, smoothly, a slow transfer of power in the middle of a fast dance. She looked into my face, and nodded, and one of her hands flew up and away, like a bird, out, flutter, then returning, to her hip. All done like it was supposed to be done just that way, no other way. As of this point, it was not quite eating at me, that I was here as a fraud. That I was, in fact, still the rat she thought I was. That, if she knew the truth . . . ooohh, let's not go there. Let's go back. Her face. Sally's neat unblemished peach-colored confident face showed nothing that shouldn't occur to a face on a dance floor. You could not tell she was thinking about dancing, the way I was sure you could see the whole complicated process on my furrowed, sweaty brow. You could not see calculations or pressures or who's-looking-at-me on Sally's face, because it was apparent that Sally did not care. You could not see that I had told a lie about Sally, and that there were probably a lot of people in that hall thinking about that lie at that minute. Why couldn't you see that? I would expect to see that.

"I suppose I deserved it . . . a little," Sally said, looking off over my head as she said it. "I pulled one on you, you pulled one on me. Now that we're all clear, we're square."

Oh. Ow.

I stopped dancing. I stood flat-footed and, I guess, stared at her. Reality, just when you're getting the engine started up on your denial, is a cold shot. We were not all clear. We were not square.

"I'm still pulling one," I said, not loud enough to be heard over the music.

But loud enough to be heard by my mentor. "Excuse us," Frankie said, bumping me, manhandling me off the dance floor while both of our partners continued dancing without us. He hustled me all the way to the snack table, where Mikie was.

"Talk some sense to this guy," Frank said to Mike as he grabbed himself a drink. "He listens to you. Tell him not to blow it with Sally."

Mike cracked a huge cookie in half, gave me the smaller piece. "Okay. El, don't blow it with Sally."

Frank finished his drink, made a snort noise. "Fine," he said. "I got business. Can't be wasting my time. . . ." And he was gone back to the dance floor.

"I'm afraid I'm disappointing him," I said. But as I said it, I realized I couldn't manage to care. "I'm going to tell the truth about Sally. I meant to already, but got sidetracked. Anyway, know what? Know what's weird, Mike?"

Mikie waited. This was an old, old story. The difference was, this time I was *saying* it was weird before he had to tell me.

"I'm not, like, all upset that Sally's not gonna like me. Even though she's great and every guy probably wants to go out with her."

He turned to look her way. There she was, still dancing, but not by herself anymore. I looked at the guy dancing with her and thought, for no good reason, Ah, she could do better. She could have . . .

"Hey," I said, "why don't you talk to her? Now *that*

makes sense." The more I thought about it, the more sense it did make. "Ya. Right. That's what bothers me, I think. I don't fit there. But you do. Interested?"

Mikie continued looking, started smiling, looked interested. Then turned to me.

"Nope," he said, shrugging.

That appeared to be that. No, though.

"How come?" I asked, and it was surprisingly hard coming out.

"Truth?" Mikie asked me.

Simple enough proposition there. Truth. Truth? Like in, did I *want* the truth? Well, easy, no? Isn't the answer to that always yes?

No. Of course it isn't.

But.

"Yes," I said. "Truth."

Best friend I ever had. Makes a difference.

"Truth is, El, I have no idea. I mean, really, I have no idea why not." He shrugged.

It was a big shrug. Not an *I don't care, either movie is fine with me* shrug. It was more of a *no answer there, let's shelve this for now* shrug.

"What about you?" Mike asked. "What's your excuse?"

This was one of those moments, one of the million moments. Where without necessarily telling me anything, Mikie told me something. But then he told me not to pursue it, either. And so I would need to tell him something too. Not as a trade, but as a *want*.

I scanned the place, suddenly, madly, seeking. I put a hand on Mike's shoulder so he could be ready when I wanted to force him to see what I saw. Then my eyes rested, off to the side, just off the main dancing area of the floor, where that girl, the round-faced curlicue girl who would not tell me her name, where she passed by with a cookie and a Kool-Aid.

"That's the girl I can't stop thinking about," I said.

He looked at her. Looked at her, nodded, then looked at me.

"So *don't*," he said.

Right there. That was the moment. If Mikie said so, I knew I was right.

"Help me," I said.

"No way." He backed up like I had yet another creepy medical problem. "That's not my game. Get Frank to help."

"Impossible. Frankie had a plan for me, and I'm breaking from his plan so he's gonna be all mad. And besides . . ." It hit me then, like it was personal, like somehow I was wounded. "Frankie thinks she's . . . I don't know. Not quite. Not, like, *enough*, or something."

Mikie looked at her one last long time, over there munching her cookie.

He was gentle with me. "Or that she's a little *more* than enough?" he said.

I nodded.

Like a human bulldozer, he circled behind me and plowed me toward the round-faced girl of my dreams.

What was it about these dances? If I could get the girls to manhandle me the way the guys did . . .

There was no great surprise on her face when we finally reached her. We were pretty obvious. "Hi," Mikie said confidently from over my shoulder. Maybe that's what I should have done, come in with a human shield.

"Hi," she said.

"My name's Mike, and this is Elvin."

"Hi. My name's Barbara."

Wow. Mikie was *great* at this.

He didn't have to shove me anymore, so he stood back and let me waver on my own. She seemed somehow friendlier now, softened somewhat. We stood for a minute or so grinning at each other kind of stupidly. At least hers was stupid. Mine I couldn't see, but I could assume.

The time of my life. That's exactly what it was.

"What are you *doin'*, Elvin?" Frank asked. Accused, really. He pulled on my arm, making me spill splotches of pink sugar water all over the varnished floor. I didn't even realize I had a drink in my hand.

"Shaddup, Franko, is what I'm doing. Get outta here." I yanked my arm back, spilled most of what was left of my drink.

"All our hard work . . . you were on the brink. You were a couple of rungs away from climbing out of the dry well of your sorry little life." He made a big showy gesture in the direction of Sally, like he was a magician and was about to saw her in half. "*Sally*, for god's sake, El. Remember Sally?"

"I'm thirsty," Barbara said, and walked away. In the opposite direction from the drinks table.

"Now look what you did, bonehead," I said.

Frank was about to respond when Mikie—who apparently found something he liked to do at dances—started muscling him away. "You're on your own now," Mike said.

"Good," I said, and scurried off to find Barbara.

If this was a movie, you know, where things work out right and the music matches every mood and the backgrounds never get in the way of the action, and when you want dreamy or sad or romantic you get dreamy or sad or romantic, then I would have found Barbara outside the gym, leaning on a fresh-waxed copper-colored convertible or under a young maple tree, kicking at the roots with her toe. And either way, the dance music would settle down on us like a friendly warm mist that just visited and didn't disturb anything.

But it was not a movie. It was my real life.

I found Barbara sitting on the edge of the auditorium stage, her back against one throbbing speaker as something scary—the Beach Boys or something—fell out of it. We had to scream at each other.

"Hey," I said.

"Hey."

"I thought I lost you."

"Your friend is a dirtbag."

"Oh," I said, reaching back into the mental file of all the times I'd had to try and explain Frankie to people. "Well, no, Frankie, he's not a dirtbag. He's just . . . handsome."

I shrugged. Somehow, I just expected her to understand that. The way I pretty much always had. I hoped, hoped, anyway, that it would work that way. Boy, did I need her to understand.

She nodded. She did, did understand.

Mostly.

"He can be both, you know," Barbara said, still nodding.

She got me nodding. I got her grinning. The reflective white crescents of her cheeks again came up and arced high above where any cheekbone could follow. Her eyes hid again behind them. I think I sighed.

"What?" she asked. The music was still swamping us, but still leaving me audible apparently.

"You *heard* that?" I asked.

"I heard *something* come out of you, but I don't know what it was exactly. That's why I said, 'What?'"

Good, she didn't hear it. Gotta be cool. Sighing like that so soon wouldn't be cool. Good, good, she missed it, that was a close one. Whew.

"What?"

"Nothing. Did I say 'whew'? Sorry. Nothing." Jeez, how long have I been going around saying everything I think? Dangerous trend there. How lame am I that I didn't know? Why didn't anybody tell me?

The song changed. Thank goodness. Crap. More surfer music. I could swear it was the same song if they hadn't stopped the music, paused, and started up again. The dopes.

"I love these old beachy songs," Barbara said, starting to sway.

"Absolutely," I said, starting to sway.

The one of us who was telling the truth even closed her eyes to love the music an extra bit. I realized how hard I was staring at her when I felt my eyelids pulling down along with hers.

But I caught them just in time. To some jolt in the tune, some spasm of rhythm or melody that I could not hear but that oh boy could I appreciate all the same, Barbara toggled.

Toggled. Her head, her rounder than earth, smoother than ice cream face tilted this way then that, back this way then again. The curls, hanging lower, shinier with the heat, brushing her cheek, touching her shoulder, falling around her eyes until with two dimpled hands she swept the whole hairy killing me dead mess back up and over and out of her way again.

Out of *my* way.

She did it two or three quick times, the toggle, as if she were trying to shake something out of her ears, and the effort didn't trouble her one bit.

Troubled *me*. Troubled me crazy.

She caught me, and god only knows what a sweaty

pervert I must have looked like because she immediately shrank away from me, leaning all the way back into the speaker, sinking there like into a wingback chair.

Merely startled, however. She toggled once more. A gift. And you know why? Because she had no idea she was giving it to me. She was just enjoying herself. And I was just enjoying herself.

"I love it because it makes me think of nothing," Barbara said, referring to the sounds swirling around her head. "The surf stuff. It makes me think of just nothing, and I like my music to do that. A good feeling for no good reason."

And so. I stood, still and silent and sappy, staring up at her there. And just as I was learning to love the surf, after I had already gotten the good feeling for what I thought was a pretty darn excellent reason, they pulled the plug. Just like that. Music over. Dance over.

And though I knew it made no sense, I felt like *everything* was over. When the lights came up—they weren't very down to begin with—a panic filled my belly and I wanted to make a sound like a seagull.

I at least managed not to do that. But . . .

"I have puppies," I said as I awkwardly rushed the stage to help Barbara with the short trip down. Where do I put my hands? Do I speak? Here, Barbara, let me grab something? Here, Barbara, grab onto me. Or hell, I should just drop to the floor and let her bounce off me like a moon walk. I'd do it, if that were the thing. What was the right thing for a guy to do here?

By the time I'd finished bumbling, of course, she was down off the stage, with her back toward me. She never even knew I was being gallant.

"Puppies?"

"Ya, a whole bunch of them. Wanna see 'em, Barbara? You can have one. You can have more than one, even. They're really sweet. And they're beautiful." Please god, this'll be my final lie, don't strike me down. . . .

I waited ten seconds. No lightning. Oh well, good. Maybe I could paint them or something before she came over.

"BB."

"Huh?"

"It's what my friends call me. Not Barbara. Although you can still call me Barbara if you prefer."

Dropkick me Jesus, I was now all the way intimate, with such a pretty girl. *Such* a pretty girl. I didn't know what Frankie was thinking, what he thought was a pretty girl but . . . holy smokes, I kept feeling like I wanted to reach out and just put a hand on her face like they tell you you can't do to the artwork in the museum.

"Whoa, you okay there, Elvin Bishop?" Barbara asked, grabbing my elbow just before I lost my footing entirely.

Did you hear that? the way she said all of my name, just like that?

"Ya, thanks, I just slipped in some bug juice there. Dangerous stuff, y'know?" I paused. A spastic pause. Followed by a blurt. "*Barbara*, though."

"Huh?"

"Barbara, I think is prettier. Than BB. Suits you better. It's what I would call you . . . y'know, if you were letting me call you something."

"And I will call you Elvin, unless you prefer something else."

I'd answer to anything. So I just nodded.

I stood outside as the sisters of our sister school were shoved back on their bus. I waved, and was waved at. I smiled, and was smiled at. She blinked. I heard it—the swoosh of her eyelashes. I waved again, just a small, doofus wave to see if it was real, if I could get one back again. I did. I looked around to see who could see but, funny enough, they all had their own stuff to see.

I wanted to make the bus stay. I wanted to keep Barbara there in the parking lot. Or to accompany them, running alongside the bus, beneath her window. Just to talk. Or to listen would be fine.

And not to make one single joke, even.

RARE
COMPANY

Life, I would dare to say, was on the upswing.

Physically, I was just a shadow of the Elvin I once was. I felt strong and lean. I didn't want to eat every minute because, to my surprise, I found there was other stuff to do. And when I had to get from point a to point b, I walked rather than slunk.

And I barely suffered the slightest lingering effects of my old, debilitating medical issue.

Love can work miracles.

Okay, love *and* EXTREME UNCTION.

So I used it, all right? I don't know what the secret was—and judging from Darth's manner and his references to the import trade, I probably don't want to know—but I don't think a visit with the Pope could have been as transforming as my private anointings with UNCTION.

So it was only right. I had to settle up two scores. I had to pay for The Cure, and I had to once-and-for-all come clean on the Sally lie. I stopped hiding from Darth in bathrooms and lockers and teachers' lounges, all of which was pretty much of a joke anyway since the Witness Protection Program couldn't hide you from him if he really wanted you.

I wasn't even afraid. Maybe the magic ingredients of EU had seeped all the way up to my brain.

"Mr. Sphinc, what are you, stuck up now? You can't talk to your comrades? Just because you've achieved a certain status with the ladies, you don't know anybody anymore?" This was the man himself talking.

"Huh?" I was walking down the steps headed for the cafeteria, but when Darth gently nudged me toward the exit, I went with the flow. Outside, with the sun shining on my head, I got somehow woozier, breezier, easier. We sat in the grass.

Silently I drew the twenty-dollar bill out of my pocket, the one my mother had given me for the vet appointment I ditched. In a way, yes, I kind of stole it, but I reasoned that Ma was pretty well attached to me by now, and me being dead in the filthy river might upset her more than the twenty.

"This is just part of it, I know. But—and by the way, it really, really works—"

"I can tell by the way you're sitting," he said, satisfied with his work. "I love doing things for humanity."

"But I'm working on getting you the rest—"

Darth held up a hand. "I don't want to talk about that now. I know you'll make it up to me, one way or another."

You heard that, right? So I'm not paranoid. There

was something a little unsettling just happened around the second part of that statement, right?

"Hey," he said, clapping his hands. "Are you listening to me?"

"Sorry, shoot. I mean, continue."

"I just wanted to say, that word's out on you, boy."

Oh boy. Now I remembered the scary stuff.

"People are quite impressed with you. The way you're leading the league in girlfriends, getting all buff and such. This is turning the heads of some very important folks."

I was way beyond being able to speak to any of this. Anyway, I don't think I was expected to.

"Congratulations," he said, and then, inexplicably, punched me in the shoulder hard enough to tip me over backward into the grass.

I lay on my back, squinting into the sun. "Was that a good beating you just gave me, or something I should be worried about because you're just getting started?"

He laughed. "I swear, Sphinc, you don't know how to not be funny."

"I could learn," I said quickly. "You want me to learn? Gimme like a minute, and I swear . . ."

Just then, Metzger, who must have seen us through the glass doors of the school, came flying out into the yard. "Go on, Darth," he screamed, like you do when you're in a crowd watching a fight, only it sounds particularly stupid when the crowd is one guy. "Hit him again. Finish him. Kick his ass. Don'tcha *hate* him . . .

thinks he's so damn funny . . ."

All nine feet and seven hundred and fifty very hard pounds of Darth stood up now, throwing a shadow over Metzger, and me, and half the cars in the parking lot.

"He *is* damn funny," Darth said, in a voice that sounded like god's father.

This was a moment I could enjoy. Except it didn't rightfully belong to me. It was like at the dance when Sally was easing up on me, saying we were square, dancing with me because she thought I'd done the right thing.

"You want me to kill him, Sphinc?"

In my mind we were starting to blend, me and Metzger. Like Darth beating Metz was not really different from Darth beating me, just a matter of time.

Blended too, like being Darth's friend—or his pet, or his court jester or whatever I was—and being his victim. It wasn't hard to feel both at the same time.

What to do? Metzger, the bully. Bane of my unspectacular-as-it-is existence. Menace. Stood there shaking, eyes closed, apparently praying—praying, right there in the midday sun—with at least three different very obvious wetnesses appearing on his body that were not there when he ran through that door a few minutes earlier.

But Metzger, who was at least being Metzger. In his cavemanlike integrity, doing his thing. While I was what?

I'll give you a hint. I was dying one of my thousand deaths as I thought about it.

144

"That's okay, Darth," I said. "I think I'd rather see you not."

Darth started to laugh, did a double take. "What?"

"He wants you to let me g-g-g-go," Metzger whispered.

"Oh," Darth sneered. "Then, g-g-g-*go!*"

And g-g-go he did, three times as fast as he ran on the way out.

Darth sat back down, cross-legged, and like he was wiping a blackboard clean, proceeded as if Metzger had never been there.

"By the way, speaking of your gut . . . it's a little smaller, if I'm not mistaken. Your girlfriends must love that."

I didn't think we had been speaking of my gut, but sometimes it just sort of involves itself in the conversation.

Momentarily thrown. "Ya think so?" I asked, tugging my shirtfront down tight over my bod. "Wait, my girl-whats?"

"Can't even keep track, with the old mad social whirl you've got swinging. And that's why, that and the joking, why you're in rare company."

Did you hear something in there? Something just a little bit scary again? Ya, so did I. We do need to stay alert when talking with this guy, no?

"Rare company?"

"You betcha. Only two freshmen have *ever* been at any of my parties. One's Frankie. The other's you."

Darth extended a hand like he was going to do that buddy thing I've seen guys do, where they help each other up off the ground simultaneously. I had always admired that move, and now . . .

He shook my hand. "Saturday night. Ten o'clock."

Holy smokes, this was a lot. "Sure," I said. "I just have to, you know, check with my mom . . ."

You know how sometimes you'll say something and before the words have even had time to reach the other person . . . I was grabbing at those stupid words, could see them, in balloony cartoony print.

He was pretty darn stunned. "Check with your mo—" He stopped himself. He pointed at me and said, "Ahhhh," as if we were sharing a great joke. "You never stop, do ya, ya friggin' goof," he said.

"Friggin' goof," I said, throwing my hands up in the air. "Like you said, I just don't know how to not be funny."

And a sudden, very reasonable panic overtook me. I was getting in deeper and deeper and deeper here and it seemed the closer I got to telling Darth what I really really needed to tell him, the harder it got to actually do it. Rare company, for godsake. I couldn't enter rare company with this black spot on my record. This had to be fixed, or bad things . . . "I got to tell you—"

"You will bring your date, or dates," he said, getting to his feet, dusting off his backside. "You can bring as many as you want, as long as one of 'em is that Sally girl, right?"

Shiiiit. Shit shit shit.

He glared at me. "Nobody's ever said that to one of my invitations before."

"Oh," I gasped. "Oh, oh, no. I sat on a rock, is all. Didn't mean to say anything. Party sounds great."

"Cool. You started to tell me something before?"

"Huh? Oh. That? Oh . . . right. You like puppies? I was thinking I could pay you in—"

"No. Don't like puppies. See you Saturday." Darth headed back toward school, where in all likelihood they were holding off lunch just for him. "Ten o'clock, don't forget."

Forget? Ah, probably not.

BREAD

"Parpies?" Barbara asked. "Putties? Elvin, I'm having trouble understanding you."

I was handling the telephone with even more mastery than usual. Easy, boy. Calm. Breathe. Better. Girls like it when a guy can breathe.

"Puppies," I said, very calm, very breathy. Good, don't start with the party thing. What kind of animal calls a girl for the first time and invites her to a filthy late-night orgy. That's like second-date stuff.

Puppies, though. Puppies are another thing entirely. Puppies are the opposite of orgies. Bet you didn't know that, did you?

"Hello," she said. "Hello, Elvin? Are you still there?"

Guess I was working that out for a while.

"Ya, sorry. Puppies. I wanted to know if . . . you remember, the puppies I was telling you about, at the dance . . ."

"Right, the puppies."

"Ya, the puppies . . ." I was really cruising now. This

was going very well. Much better than I'd expected. You couldn't even tell, probably, that I'd never done this sort of thing before. And just wait till her parents met me . . .

"Hello? Elvin, are you still . . ."

Whoops. "Puppies," I said.

"Yes, we've established that," Barbara responded. "Now whadya say we try laying a verb in there, huh, Elvin?"

Say. I like *that*. Peppery dame, isn't she?

"Sure. Sure, I can do that. Ah, okay, puppies . . . gotta love 'em."

Smooooth, there, Bishop. Straddle that line. Kiss them babies. Eat that apple pie. Say nothing she could possibly disagree with. "Gotta love puppies . . ."

"Make me," she said.

Make me? Make me, love puppies? Holy smokes, what kind of a devil woman had I . . . I mean, Darth not liking puppies was one thing . . . I started squirming in my seat, nowhere to go, until I heard her giggling on the line. Whew.

"Are you calling me for a date, Elvin Bishop? Or are you trying to sell me a dog?"

"Well . . . ah . . . which one would you be more likely to say yes to?" Good thing you can't hear sweat over the phone. I added a completely accidental and nervous-sounding ha-ha at the end. Dope. You never laugh at your own material. Jeez, this was so hard, *it was so hard*, why was it so hard? Like, boxing, hard. The bell, the bell, mercy where's the bell?

"Lemme go see what I have in my piggybank," she said.

That made me feel better. Good tension-breaking. Well-timed joke. God, there was something great about this person.

"Hey, good one, Bar—"

I stopped short at the sound of her actually dropping the phone on a hard surface.

"Hello?" I called hopefully. I heard her footsteps doppling away from the phone. "I can't believe this," I said out loud. "I didn't really want her to—"

Stopped short again, wouldn't you know. By more footsteps. These, however belonged to my mother, who was now bounding down the stairs.

I had not, up till this point, so much as mentioned Barbara's name to my mother, which was something even I didn't understand. Something wild was happening to me, and the more real Barbara was becoming to me, the more I felt like hiding from Ma. Not that that was possible. She knew something was up from the very first zing of the string of my heart, but I was not up to facing it. Facing her. No, facing it.

The footsteps got closer, closer. "Pick up the phone, for the love of . . . pick up . . ." I murmured to Barbara, who was probably standing there having a quick sandwich and listening to my teeth gnashing.

Ma hit the bottom step, pivoted, and came my way.

"Shit," I said.

That pried something loose. Barbara broke out in a laugh.

Ma came right up to me, acting as if she just had to get something from the kitchen. Right, how often does a person need something from the *kitchen*? Think quick, Bishop.

Bang. I half threw, half fumbled the receiver to the floor. Exactly like in the reality cop shows, when the perp throws the drugs on the ground and says, "No, sorry, that's not mine, officer."

"Hello?" The tiny, transistor radio voice came from the floor.

Oh, and don't think my mother, uncommonly comical mother that she is, didn't have herself a good old time with this.

"That for you?" she asked sweetly.

"Is what for me?" I asked, sitting tight in the telephone-table seat, doodling the name Barbara in the telephone-side notepad. Yes, at this point I did realize how I looked, but where was I supposed to go?

"Hello?" the little voice interrupted.

"Ah, that," Ma said, pointing down at the voice.

"That?" I asked, doodling mightily, casually, mighty casually. The pen had torn through the top three sheets of paper. "No, that's not for me."

"Hello?" The damn voice. "Hello, Elvin? Elvin?"

Ma didn't even smile. Oh, she's very good.

"It *thinks* it's for you," she said.

"It's *confused*," I said, leaning down toward the

151

phone, pretty much giving myself away, don't you think? "What are you laughing at, *Mother*?"

"I'm not laughing. When you are a mother it's called beaming. You're so cute. Why don't you just pick up the phone? Is it a girl? It's a girl, isn't it? Oh Lester," Ma said, looking up toward heaven, which according to all reliable information is definitely *not* where Lester is.

I pointed at the ceiling. "This is none of your concern, Lester."

"Hello?" the phone said. "I'm gonna hang up."

"Oh god, no!" Ma and I both said at the same time. We also both made a grab for the phone. She beat me.

"Well hello," Ma said, looking at me. "Yes, I am Mrs. Bishop. A pleasure to meet you, Barbara. But I'm not exactly meeting you, really, am I? We'll need to correct that. You'll come for dinner."

"Ma." I snapped. "Slow down." This was killing me. I was so embarrassed. But you didn't see me stopping her either, did you? And in the middle of it all, Ma slipped me the wink.

We both knew I could use a lot of help here. I suppose a lot of guys might not want their moms making their dates. . . .

But I'm not a lot of guys. I'm just barely *one*. And she's not your regular mom.

She slapped me on the leg, and I relinquished the telephone seat. "How's Thursday night? Excellent. Now what do you like to eat?"

I listened. Plans were made. I hovered, poised to

snatch the phone away at the first hint of an uncomfortably cute Elvin story. Nothing. All clear. Ma passed me the receiver.

"Ya," I said to Barbara. "She is. Very. Uh-huh. No, you're right, it's pretty much round-the-clock fun around here. . . ."

Ma gave me the A-OK sign and skipped off to the kitchen.

"So," I said tentatively, "it's, like, done then? You and Ma, you made a date?"

She hesitated. "Kind of sounds different when a boy's mother says it. Less serious, you know? But now . . ."

I panicked, thinking I was losing her. "You want me to put Ma back on the line?"

I could hear her relax, which made me relax. Sort of.

"You're a hoot, Elvin."

"That's good, right?"

"That's good. So I guess . . . you think? This is a date, what we'd call this thing?"

I practically whispered. "If you wouldn't mind that."

"I wouldn't mind," she repeat-whispered. I'd never heard anything like that sound, and never felt anything like what it did to me. Like she was biting right into my chest.

I said good-bye then, without firming up plans, without setting a time, without telling her how to get here or asking where I could meet her. Because that I could do later. If I lost my mind and babbled and thanked her and cried and sang "It Had to Be You," like

I was sure I was about to, there probably would be no later.

So I sat, stupid and safe, smiling and serene, over the lifeless telephone. I breathed it in, as if she were coming through the line.

"Yoo hoo," Ma called from the kitchen.

Like waving ammonia under my nose.

"No," I said, and started for the stairs. "You're going to tease me."

"Come on now, Elvin, don't be like that. Come in here; we need to talk."

I had to concede that she was right. I could hardly pull off a dinner without her cooperation. But I knew she was going to make me squirm.

When I entered the kitchen, she was hunched at the table in that inscrutable pose of card players and movie detectives. Elbows propped on Formica, hands cradling and blocking most of the face, leaving just eyes exposed, squinting from amusement, or pain, or confusion, or a million other things. We could presume humor in this case.

I sat across from her and did the smart defensive thing, assuming the same pose. I stared at her.

She stared at me. I wasn't going to give her anything. I'm good. But she is better. She taught me everything I know, and I knew that any second she was going to reduce me to a puddle on the floor. All in good fun, of course.

The pause was unbearable.

She dropped her hands.

"What do you think? Stroganoff?" she asked pensively. "I think Stroganoff makes a nice impression. We want to make a nice impression, because she sounds like a really nice girl."

I waited. Ma and I had a sort of unspoken arrangement: We never went more than a couple of minutes without at least one of us cracking wise. At least since Lester took the Big Victory Lap, or the BVL as we called it (see?), that was always how we did it. But this was real. This was touch-and-go here.

"I think whatever you think, Ma. I think you'll know all the right things to do."

"Well," she said, "I don't know, Elvin. It's not as if you provide me a lot of occasions to practice my hostessing skills."

Ah, that's more like it.

I stood, leaving her scribbling madly with a stubby little pencil on a four-by-six notepad. "Artichoke hearts," she muttered. "Artichoke hearts are nice." She looked very happy.

"Ma," I said, turning around in the doorway. "Now remember, when she's here, if you can't control yourself you can make a joke about me here and there. But absolutely no naked baby pictures, right?" Don't ask me why, but there's no known photograph of me wearing clothes until I reached school age.

"Oh, Elvin. Not even the one where you took Mr. Potato Head and—"

"*Especially* not the one where I took Mr. Potato Head and . . ."

She didn't answer. She didn't need to. Just went back to working her shopping list, and I went back to watching her. This really was something different, a new look, a variation on Ma. Maybe I really had never given her a shot at this.

She was all right, my ma. And I thought I just might tell her. And get it over with. But watch closely now or you might miss it.

"Hey," I said. "You know what?"

"What?" She did not look up.

"Lester did all right for himself."

"Better than all right," she concurred.

"I hope eventually I make as good a choice as Lester made."

"What choice?" she asked. "We were so drunk, you were four months old before we even realized we were married."

Now, she looked up. "Scali bread, or baguette?"

"Baguette," I answered, nodding several times more than that question required. The traditional end of a Bishop Family Moment, talking about *something else*.

Good thing Ma and I both speak bread.

STROGANOFF

It was the day. *The* day. I survived waking up and eating and walking and Ma and school well enough, but survived it was all I did. Barbara just kept growing in my mind, and as she did, everybody else kept shrinking, all my other concerns kept melting. I knew enough to be slightly ashamed of myself, feeling like I was doing something intimate and private in public. Had to keep to myself. But also had to prepare.

The dogs. Jeez, the puppies. I'd promised Barbara cute puppies, but all I had were *these*. Right after school I went to the garage, and spent time with them, as if somehow attention was going to improve them.

I picked up one puppy. The vet said whenever we picked up a puppy, we were to bring it around to the mother's nose, so she could sniff it, sniff us, see that everything was okay.

"Here, Grog," I said, offering the offering.

Grog opened his eyes without raising his head. Saw the child. Closed the eyes, tight, like he was wincing.

"Ya," I said, "you *should* be embarrassed. And you're a lousy mother too, boy."

So I didn't bother asking permission anymore. One by grisly one I picked up the entire litter—now there's an accurate term—sizing them up, holding them by the window light, holding them *away* from the light, turning them at different angles, fixing their uniformly olive-colored hair this way and that to somehow work with their best features. I had bought a soft-bristle dog brush that afternoon. So there I was, holding this bug-eyed, oily, black-tongued, completely nostrilless Chia Pet in one hand while with the other I was brushing away madly trying to get its bangs to fall rakishly over one eye and maybe score us a point or two for rugged good looks.

Rugged we got, at least. The hair that grew on the pups' faces was so hard and wiry, growing straight out in all directions from around the eyes, the sagging cheeks, and the double chins, it was as if we were acupuncturing them. On the bright side, I was able to bend and twist the face hairs into decorative shapes.

"See," I said when I finished molding one of them, "this design I made here, this is what a *dog* is shaped like. Ever seen that shape before?"

I was talking to them out there in the garage. I was getting like Marlon Brando and his birds in *On the Waterfront*.

"You're not even trying," I said to the lot of them when I had finished after two hours. I'd arranged them just so on the floor with their mother and they looked exactly like they had when I arrived. "This is important to me, you guys. We're trying to make a good impression here." Predictably, the dogs were unmoved. "She's not even gonna want to eat, after she sees you."

"Elvin," Ma called from the house, "Barbara's here."

Yow. Hey stomach, what's that for? Settle down. There was no reason she wouldn't be here now. That was the plan. Barbara would walk the several blocks to my house, and I would walk her home.

I poked my head out the garage door, and looked to the kitchen window where Ma was.

"Elvin," she said calmly, "will I send her out there?"

"No!" I yelled, both hands stuck way out in front of me.

I scurried back to the dogs, fluffed them up like pillows, turned, and trotted up to the house.

When I banged through the door, I was not prepared. My life had not prepared me for this one, or anything like it.

I saw her like I had somehow not managed to see her before.

Barbara had on a dress, for godsake. It was red. No, it was green, a deep forest green, or pink. Made of velvet, or was it fishnet.

Anyway, the point is, it was girl shaped, and merciless. She looked so . . . pretty. That doesn't sound like much, I suppose, when a guy like me is just saying it and you're not seeing it, but it is much. It is a lot of much.

Pretty. I mean, my mother is pretty. My yard is pretty late in the spring and early in the fall, but we're not talking about that and you know it. I mean *pretty*. And it does not come in, all the way in, to a guy's life all that often, does it?

At least not into mine.

"Hi, Elvin," she said, opening up a heartlessly heart-shaped, red-framed smile on me. She had just a little bit of lipstick on.

I grabbed onto the nearby radiator for support. Then I waved casually with the other hand to make it look more suave than desperate. "Hi," I ad-libbed.

Ma stood there, looking us over. She held out a small bunch of flowers, wildflowers, purple and gold and white, that had obviously been recently and locally picked, wrapped in crinkly white tissue and tied with a fat length of royal-blue yarn. "Look what Barbara brought me," she said.

We were already well beyond my experience with stuff like this, so I had no idea what kind of response I was supposed to make. Fortunately, neither did Barbara. We looked at each other. Shrugged, smiled.

"Excellent home training," Ma silently mouthed at me. You wouldn't necessarily expect to be able to lip-read such a thing under this kind of pressure from halfway across a room, except that it is a sort of standard thing when she meets a new person. A positive reference to the individual's home training is a gold star on the forehead.

"This was so nice of Barbara," Ma said, since nobody

else was willing to talk. "I think she deserves a puppy for this."

Go, Ma. We had been working madly, trying to unload the puppies all around town.

"Ya," I said, because that's what I always said. But then I remembered that I actually *liked* Barbara. "No, but . . . we should eat first," I said, slamming the door behind me for don't-go-there emphasis. I'd have piled furniture up against the door if it weren't so conspicuous.

"Ah, no," Ma said, turning to the cupboard to find a pitcher for her flowers. "There's time yet. Go on out to the garage."

"Shit," I blurted.

They both looked at me with the identical one-brow-raised expression.

"I mean, shshshsh . . . *shtep* right this way, miss." I threw open the door, just as if I really wanted her to walk through it. And so she did. When Barbara was out and heading down the stairs, I could let my face sink to where it belonged. What was I going to do about this? Ma grinned at me insanely and gave me the thumbs-up as if one of us had just won the Daytona 500. She was no help.

"Please," I said as we both turned toward our respective duties, "don't do that."

I caught up to Barbara as we neared the garage, and I started thinking spin control. I flashed on the last view I had of the pups and their mother, all gathered together and oozing like a big 3-D oil splotch on the garage floor.

"Shit," I said.

"You have, like, a tic or something," Barbara asked, "makes that word come out of you for no reason?"

We had reached the garage. I scooted ahead of her and stood with my back to the door, barring her entry. "I have to be honest with you before we go in there," I said.

"Is this about you and your mother? I've heard the stories, but frankly I just found them too unbelievable to be taken seriously."

I waved my hands at her. "No, it's about"—I swallowed, pointed over my shoulder. "It's about the pups. These are not—" I stopped. I'd been listening in slow motion because I was thinking in fast motion. "What *about* me and my mother? Who's talking about—"

"Are you going to let me see these puppies or not? Jeez, Elvin, the way you go on, it's like you have an insane relative hiding in your garage or something."

"I wish. Okay. Let me just tell you, these are not . . . handsome dogs. I don't want you to go in there and think, like, we've been mutilating them, or that they were part of some kind of sick genetic manipulation. . . ."

Barbara reached out then, and put her hand flat on my chest.

She put her hand flat on my chest.

She put, her hand, flat on my chest.

All seven of my hearts accelerated at once. Inside me it sounded and felt like a helicopter squadron. From that moment on, I didn't care what was waiting in the garage. In fact, all I knew then about the garage was that it was holding me up. And I was alone with Barbara.

"You're so funny." She left her hand on me as she spoke. "All puppies are adorable. Some are just a little less adorable, and some are more, that's all. Now, are you going to let me in there?"

I gave it some thought. As much thought as I was at that moment capable of.

"Go in where?" I asked, without meaning to be funny or cute or anything.

"Hah," Barbara laughed, and pushed me aside.

When she'd passed, I put my hand into the exact spot where her hand had just been, flat on my chest. I could swear I felt the handprint, still warm. Her hand was exactly the same size as mine.

"Oh my *god*," she yelped from inside.

Oh ya. The puppies.

When I reached her, she was pacing back and forth in front the sleeping knot of mutts, trying to get a different angle on them.

"Don't bother," I said. "It doesn't get any better."

"What did you mate her with, Elvin, a pineapple?"

"Hey, *I* didn't mate her with anything. I didn't even know he was a girl."

The one-eyebrow-stare again. "Didn't come with the instruction manual, I guess, huh?"

Boy, she reminds me of somebody.

Barbara looked away from me, stood there for a

minute with her hands on her hips looking hard at the dogs. They must have felt the heat of her glare, because they got all in an uproar. One of them stretched. One of them opened its eyes. One wild thing actually got to its feet, without opening its eyes, took a couple of steps, then reconsidered and went back to sleep.

"They are cute," Barbara said.

"What?"

"Cute. I said they are cute." She didn't even sound like she needed to convince herself, though that appeared to be just what she had been doing. She'd accomplished it already.

"You can't believe that," I said.

"I can. And I do," she responded. And as if to prove it, she went right to the pile and extracted not one but two of the dogs. Without gloves on even.

To distinguish one pup from another I had come up with a system of identifying them in terms of pasta colors, textures, and thicknesses, according to the design of the hair that shot out from their faces. Barbara was holding the one with the #2 whole wheat linguine face and the one with the squid-ink tagliatelle face.

"No offense, Barbara," I said, "but I think you're a little reckless with the way you use the word *cute*."

She looked up from actually nuzzling the two animals. "No accounting for taste, I guess."

Picture me now, whistling down out of the sky, barrel-rolling nose-first toward the earth with smoke coming out of my tail.

"But I happen to think I have excellent taste," she added.

And pulling right up out of that nosedive, once again sky-bound.

This was an unbelievable person here. She saw the cuteness of those beasts. And the cuteness of this one.

But just between you and me, I was getting a little nervous about the way I rose and fell on Barbara's words. She had such a control over my emotions. Way more than I had over my own.

"You said I could have one, right?" she asked.

"What? Oh, the pups. Sure. You can have one if you want. You can have them all if you want."

She nodded. "One." She bounced the two she was holding, as if judging them by weight. She looked back down at the rest, considered, then concentrated on the two in hand again.

"Does this little guy have a name?" she asked, holding Tagliatelle a little higher and nuzzling his nose with hers. He actually came to life, licking her and taking little bites of the tip of her nose. I was jealous.

"Does the little guy have a name?" I repeated. "I wasn't even sure the little guy was a little guy. But, well, ya, I was calling him Tag."

"Want to come home with Barbara, Tag?"

I call *myself* Tag, too, I thought, can I come home with Barbara? But I figured that might be a little forward to say out loud.

"Elvin!" Barbara said, eyes wide. "That was very fresh."

Oh my god, it came out of me. I covered my mouth with my hand, and the rest of my face with blush. Shit!

"Elvin!" She gasped again. Thank god she was laughing at me.

I was really no good at this, no good at all.

"I'm sorry," I said, because of my excellent home training. And then I broke into a fit of honesty, because of my lousy romantic training. "These things are happening . . . just 'cause I like you a real lot." I could feel that I was squinting very hard as I said it, as though I was anticipating a hard blow.

"Jeez, I can't imagine what you'd scream at me if you *didn't* like me a real lot," Barbara said, looking at her new dog as she spoke, which made it easier on me. "I'm taking Tag, okay?"

Before I could tell Barbara just how okay that was, how okay *everything* was, Ma called me again from the window.

"What?" I yelled, a little irritably.

"The rest of them are here," she sang.

"What?" I ran to the garage door and stared up at my mother in her window. "What are you talking about, the *rest* of them? This is it. We *are* the rest of them."

"Don't get huffy with me, Bishop," Ma said, though she didn't sound angry at all. "You're not the one trying to prepare a meal for X number of dinner guests."

"What X number?" I asked. "Three? Three is not an X number. We are only having—"

"Hey guy," Frankie said, putting his arm around my

mother's shoulders in the window. "What're you doing down there when the food's all up here?"

Ma removed Frankie's arm. He put it back. She moved it again.

"I'll be right up," I growled, pointing a finger at Frankie.

When I went back into the garage, steaming, confused, ready to blow a gasket, I came upon Barbara crouched down among the dogs, holding Tag in her lap while the others sort of mingled about around her. She was talking to them, asking them their names, telling them one by one that they were "pretty boys. Yes you are, aren't you. And pretty girls, yes." And when she would speak to one, it would turn its unfortunate little mug up toward her and react. They were wagging too, at the sound of her voice. Not that they had actual tails, more like hairy shot glasses attached to their backsides, and when they wagged them it was really that they were wagging the entire rear third of their bodies. I couldn't believe it. It looked *cute*. She got them to be cute.

I had no idea what the correct emotional response was to this situation, but I can tell you what *my* response was.

Fear. I could not stop staring at Barbara, as she coolly improved all my surroundings, and I felt afraid, that somehow this was not going to work, to be, to last. That I was not up to this. That I was not meant for this.

And all I could think to do was to kiss her for it. To

run up and kiss her, then to run away while it was still perfect. The urge was so strong . . .

"Elvin!" The call from the kitchen again.

"We gotta go," I sighed to Barbara.

"Sure," she said. "But why do you say it like that? Is your mom, like, a lousy cook or something?"

"No, she's great," I said. "It's just that we have party crashers up there now and . . ." I looked at her, and she was looking back at me intensely, waiting on my next words, taking my concern seriously. "And," I said firmly, but in reality I was in the process of chickening out. Because what I wanted to say was, I want to stay right here in the garage with you. But what I did say was, "I might have to get tough with them."

The thinking being, I guess, if you can't be smart or honest, be macho.

"Oh, Elvin," she said, shoving me hard toward the house, "you're such a goof."

Well then. Guess we'll scratch *macho* off the list of approaches.

When we got to the kitchen, Ma was busy putting out extra place settings.

"Stop that, Ma," I said. She continued without responding.

Frankie walked through the kitchen door. "Hi," he said.

"No," I said, pointing at him.

Mike walked in. "Hi."

"No."

168

"You two," I barked, one last shot at the macho. "Out in the hall."

As I followed the guys out of the kitchen, I stopped and placed a hand lightly on Barbara's arm. "Don't worry," I said. "I'll handle this."

I meant serious business now out in the hall.

"Please," I begged. "Please, guys, get outta here. This is hard enough for me. I'm like, ready to lay eggs out there in the kitchen as it is, so I know if you two rats are here I'm gonna totally waste myself with Barbara."

I was out of breath already. It was their turn.

"You got it backward," Frankie said. "I'm only here to help you. To supervise. To make sure you don't do anything you might regret later. To protect you from yourself."

"But don't let that worry you. I'm here to provide balance," Mikie added. "I'm here to supervise *him*. If you're lucky, we'll cancel each other out and you can get on with your business."

Something awfully close to a whimper slipped out of me there. As if this wasn't already ten times more complicated than anything I'd ever attempted before. I was now going to have to operate with these two being like on TV when a person has the little good guy on one shoulder whispering in his ear, and the little bad guy on the other.

"And if your mother didn't think we could be helpful, she wouldn't have invited us, right?"

"I never invited you," Ma replied from the kitchen.

They could hear us.

Oh god, they could *hear* us. "Shit."

"Elvin!" Ma said.

I headed into the kitchen again, to find the two women seated at the beautiful dinner. The table was a little crowded, but it just looked more lavish that way.

"He says that all the time," Barbara said. "He's got a little problem there, I think, Mrs. Bishop."

"It's his only one, Barbara," Mrs. Bishop said. "Otherwise he is just about perfect."

That sounded like a joke, didn't it? Could the naked baby pictures be far behind? Me and Mr. Potato Head over dessert, you'll see.

However, there was a bright spot. Barbara was looking at me, so sweetly, so—friendly, is the word—that I stopped worrying that I'd ruined myself by shooting off my mouth.

Stopped worrying about anything, really. Even Mikie and Frankie.

"You did so invite us," Frankie said to my mother, breaking like a thousand etiquette rules by engaging in an argument with the hostess, homeowner, cook, and best friend's mother.

"I never did. I merely told you that Barbara was coming for dinner tonight. Pass me the egg noodles, fresh kid."

The fresh kid passed the egg noodles.

"Wait a minute," I said. "What were you doing talking to him, anyway? What, you guys have this secret life that doesn't include me?"

Frank, who was seated on my side of the table, to the left, with Mikie between us, leaned over his plate to leer at me. "Practice calling me Dad," he said.

Ma, who was sitting in the seat directly across from Franko, reached out with the tongs she was about to use on the noodles. Snipped him right on the left earlobe, holding him still to give him a small slap on the right cheek. "Calling you *dead* is what we're going to practice if you don't get yourself under control."

Franko, who couldn't seem to tell the difference between being liked by a woman and being struck about the face and head by one, laughed.

"Now go get up and rinse these tongs off," Ma demanded. As soon he was out of his chair, she chuckled too.

"Anyway," Mikie said. "Back to the point. I called here yesterday, Elvin. Your mom was supposed to tell you."

I looked at her. "Mikie called," she said, shrugging and sending the noodles around the table.

"Well I hope you're satisfied," I said to both guys. Now, I realized that the fight over whether they were staying for dinner was pretty well finished, what with them actually sitting in front of quickly scribbled place cards with their names on them, nibbling bread rolls, and tucking cloth napkins into their shirts like bibs. But I wanted to take my last shot anyway. "My poor mother had to stretch and fill and patch together this meal because she wasn't prepared for—"

"Oh stop, Elvin," Ma said without looking at me. She was carefully ladling creamy beefy Stroganoff over the bed of noodles in her plate, in effect illustrating what she was about to say. "I made enough for ten people, for goodness' sake."

"Ya," I said, quickly running out of material, looking around at some pretty unsympathetic faces too. "Well, I was planning on *eating* enough for ten."

Ma made a subtle *tsk tsk* noise at me, and I shut up. Which helped move the evening along.

Because then we could eat, which was maybe the one thing everyone here at the table could do equally well. I probably had an edge, with a well-established history of scarfing down my mother's Stroganoff, her fettuccine Alfredo, her escarole soup, or smoked shoulder with the blackened honey-mustard shell. I knew her art, and could appreciate it without even touching it to my lips. But tonight we were a gang. A happy and hungry bunch of consumers, and I think we did better dealing with each other because of what the food did to us.

Mikie could not stop thanking Ma, and pointing out what aspect of each dish made him excited, asking what she had put into the water to make the baby carrots taste like pumpkin pie. Ma loved it, and told him nothing. Frankie moaned. His *other* moan, the one polite company can appreciate. There was almost no conversation during dinner that I can recall, and I suppose that sounds disgusting, but you'll need to just take my word for it that it wasn't. There were noises, single words like "wonderful" and "unbelievable" slipped in between bites, and there were nods and gestures with silverware toward the salad bowl, the bread basket, the serving bowls. But there wasn't a discussion about *anything*, really, and I was so, so grateful for that. No feeling that Barbara being here, in my house, at my table, across from me in the seating arrangement with the stupid funny sweet little place cards, was an issue at all.

Which freed me up to mostly just look at her. Her eyes, the color of honeydew melon tonight, were actually smaller than I had originally thought, and in fact they seemed to struggle, like little beings all their own, stretching up to get a peek at the outside world over the pale drumlins of her cheeks when she smiled. And she smiled every time she glanced up from her plate and caught me staring at her.

Like it was okay with her that I stared. Like it was not something that bored or annoyed or scared her. Like it wasn't something she was so used to that she would want me to stop. This alone made us a good pair, because I felt like I could do it for a long long time.

I'd be staring, crouching low and awkward to try and catch her eye, then she'd look up, do the smile thing, and almost cancel out her eyes altogether, the long fat lashes waving Help me like they were going under for the third time.

But eyes or no, how could I ever not want her to do that?

"I can't eat another bite," Barbara said, speaking for everybody and closing down the meal. "But I will anyway," she added, and took one last scoop of the main dish without the noodles, and a snap of bread for mopping the sauce. I was impressed. Here was someone who shared my philosophy that you don't stop eating just because you're not hungry anymore. But looking down at my own plate as my mother—and Frankie!—came around and started the clearing, I realized I hadn't gotten around to eating much of anything. And I still wasn't hungry.

When Ma came around and saw, I thought for sure it was going to be time for one of those gentle-yet-embarrassing commentaries on what's-up-with-Elvin, like I'd always heard when I'd eaten too much, or too fast, or eaten six helpings of turkey and no potatoes and none of stuffing, or the other way around, because I had for my entire life worn my emotions on my stomach.

She looked down at my plate, then at me, then at Barbara, then at me again.

She took my plate away with one hand, wordlessly, and gave my neck a squeeze with the other as she continued her rounds.

As Barbara's plate was swept away by Frankie—who was earning big points for minimal misbehavior with Barbara—she dabbed at the corners of her mouth with her napkin and leaned way out over the table to whisper to me. "This was really nice of your mother," she said. "And you."

I shrugged. "I suppose. Ya, thanks."

"Well I think we should do something for you two in return," she said.

"What's going on down there?" Mike asked.

"No, no," Barbara said, standing up and waving him off. "Sit there and relax. Elvin and I are just going to get the party favors."

"Favors?" I asked as I blindly followed Barbara to the door. "Favors?" Frankie said, reentering the picture. "I love favors. This is, like the coolest dinner party of my life, and that is saying something."

"What favors?" Ma asked as she came in with a silver bowl filled with Stella D'oros and Fig Newtons.

We were standing at the back door, about to exit.

"Didn't you tell them this was a theme party when you invited them to dinner?" Barbara asked.

Ma was awesome.

"Of course I told them," she hummed, nibbling the first anisette biscuit before she'd even hit the seat. "I told them when I invited them. They know that."

Ha. Their mouths hung open.

"Hey Ma, looks like you got two baby birds there, need to be fed. Pop a couple cookies in those beaks, and we'll be right back." Nice exit line, that. Except, I didn't go anywhere. I stood there in the doorway, wanting to linger in the moment, watch them. I felt sort of in control, and I had absolutely no idea why.

Barbara, who had already headed out, doubled back and grabbed me by the hand, tugging me along to the garage.

Ah right. That was it. As I stared at the pale dimpled hand holding mine, I realized why I was feeling the way I was feeling. The elevated Elvin. The thing that I didn't feel very often—or ever. She was doing it here now. You know that thing she did for the dogs, making them better, making them doggier, making them happy? She was doing it for me by plotting with me against my friends, by leaving a room with me. . . .

Why is that so thrilling, I'd like to know? In all my demented fantasies, my loony dreams and frothy schemes, I had done many spectacular and unlikely things with girls who had lots and lots of long hair and no faces. But never something as drab and nowhere as holding a hand and removing myself down the back stairs while a room full of people wondered about it at our backs.

My oh my, oh my oh my what I never knew. How this left every fantasy in the shade.

I stared at Barbara's hand and listened to her laugh, and it was a very good thing that I knew my stairs and my driveway and my yard as well as I did because my feet could have been anywhere doing anything for all the control I had over them.

She got the garage door partway up, but it was a creaky heavy old thing. "I'm going to need at least two hands for this, Elvin," she said.

I looked down and noticed I was squeezing. Hanging so tight to her free hand that the fingers were turning pink and puffy.

"Oh. Sorry," I said, awfully slowly. First I stared at the hands, as if sussing out whether to call for the jaws of life rather than just letting go. Then, I just let go.

Probably it was the comical slowness of all this that made Barbara giggle and look at me strangely. But it was her own unusualness that made her try and help me out.

"You are preoccupied, Elvin Bishop," Barbara said, and when she said it, everything stopped proceeding normally, the dogs stopped their snuffling on the other side of the door, the chatter stopped filtering out of the open kitchen window above and behind us. Traffic out on the street slowed to the point where cars still went by, but you could hear the suck of their tires on the pavement as much as you could their engines. I lost the ability to blink. Barbara, even her gestures and the movement of her mouth, slowed down just like in slo-mo film, only her voice didn't sink down into slo-mo deep-devil voice, thank god. Though even that wouldn't have changed my mind much.

"Con-cen-trate," she said, leaning close, leaning close.

Okay! I will! I will concentrate!

On what? On what, was I concentrating? Help.

I could not bear another second of this, stupid words and stupid acts coming to mind in a flood now as my self-destruct impulses started pumping extra juice. So I half dove at the garage door, and yanked it skyward so hard that the groaning old croaker shot up all the way, exerted maximum pressure on its springwork, then re-bounded hard, zooming back and crashing right back down at our feet. The dogs yelped and squealed and ran away inside.

"Easy there, butch," Barbara said.

"I'm really strong," I babbled. What a dink.

Please, Elvin, I pleaded with myself. Shut up and get out of the way, for the love of god, get out of the way. . . .

I gripped the handle of the garage door and raised it, easy this time. Worked out okay.

We went to the puppies, who were cowering as far from the door as possible. When they saw Barbara, they seemed to relax a bit, and Tag led the way to her. "This one is mine," she said, scooping him up and cuddling him.

I was staring again, and my stomach was jumping. I started feeling like I was going to lose whatever food I had managed to put down at dinner, right here on the dogs. Not that anybody would notice.

"So which ones do we give away?" she asked, perus-ing the crowd.

"All of them?"

"Listen, I can only help you so much. I'm taking one. Two dinner guests. That's three puppies, leaving you with four. That's pretty good."

"What about the mother?"

"Sorry, that one was your own mistake."

Grog looked up at me now, head tilted, one eye closed as if he was trying to understand what was being said.

"It was *not* my mistake. It was an accident. It was a plot. It was my mother, and Mikie. . . ."

And it all came rushing back to me, how Mikie had convinced my mother that I actually wanted this dog instead of the dirty-minded crap-throwing feces rhesus monkey that would have been by now like a new close friend, replacing Frankie, maybe, a lot of the same qualities only less complicated. And not a *lot* less complicated either. . . .

"Elvin?"

"That one right there," I said, with new determination. "That's Mikie's dog." I pointed to Tortellini, the dog with the circular orange face fronting the olive head, eyes permanently rolled skyward, who ran into walls time after time, as if to hone his already precious look. "Frankie gets Canelloni," the tubular one that looked like a dachshund with a sheepdog's coat. Once we'd scooped them up, and slammed the garage door behind us, I started hurrying. Took three steps at a trot, then stopped short.

Wait a minute. Now I knew what I was supposed to be concentrating on earlier.

"What?" Barbara asked.

I leaned forward, squashing the three little beasties between us, though they were good and simple enough not to say anything about it. With the face part of me,

I kind of lurched toward Barbara's face.

"What?" she asked again, pulling back just enough, from the neck up. I thought the *what* part of it should have been pretty obvious. And she seemed willing before. But maybe my approach was sort of less than appetizing.

Barbara shook her head no. I was still close enough that when she did it the curlicues that fell around the sides and the front of her face just lightly swept my face. So that even though it was no, it might as well have been yes, the way it made me feel.

"Sorry," I said, sorry and satisfied. Doing it all wrong and feelin' all right.

I headed up the driveway, not toward the back door from where we came, but toward the front.

"What are you doing?" she asked, but followed.

"I know my buddies," I said. "And they know me."

"Whatever that means," Barbara said.

But as soon as we turned the corner from the driveway to the sidewalk that ran past the front of my house, Barbara understood.

The two of them, Mikie and Frankie, were slithering out, whispering thank-yous to my mother and telling her not to bother disturbing me and Barbara.

So we crept along the five-foot chain-link fence that fronted my yard, and intercepted the slinksters just as they were backing out through the gate.

"Thank you," I said to the first, Frankie, who jumped. "So nice you could come." I stuck Canelloni in his hands.

"What am I supposed to with this thing?" Frank said, staring at it.

"Feed him seven times a day, and do not let him breed. SPCA made us promise." I gave him a slap on the back.

Barbara, from her post on the opposite side of the exit, tapped Frank on the shoulder. "It was nice meeting you again," she said. "Even if you did vote against me."

Whoa. Frankie blushed. Do I have to point out how hard it is to accomplish that? But at the same time he smiled. He looked at me, jerking a thumb at Barbara. "I suppose there are suckier girls you coulda picked," he said graciously. I shoved him on his way.

Barbara paused to nuzzle her dog. "My dad's gonna kill me," she said. "I gotta practice crying on the way home."

"Stare at the dog for a while," I said to be helpful. "They're like onions."

Mikie. Mikie walked up to the plate with dignity. Sort of like a condemned man who knows he's gonna get it anyway, so he's damned well not going to be seen whining and kicking on his way out. But also like a good sport who know's he's been bagged.

He held out his hands and squinted. "Payback's a bitch."

"So is this," I said, and gently placed his new best friend in his hands. "Her name is Tortellini."

Mikie looked at Tortellini. Tortellini looked at the sky though, god love her, she seemed to be making every effort to look at Mike.

"Got me back good," he said.

I waved and smiled as if I was on a parade float and he was in the crowd a hundred feet away. "Come again," I said sweetly.

And before he moved on, something transpired. Big, in its way, but probably a lot of not-much to the untrained eye. Mikie turned to Barbara and just sort of stood there. Stared at her. Smiled. She smiled back. They looked for all the world like two people who had known each other for a long time, and were briefly passing each other by again.

"You'll take good care of my boy?" Mike said in a goofy old-folks scold.

"Or you'll scratch my eyes out," Barbara shot back.

And that was it. Seemed to satisfy both of them. Mike turned to me before leaving. "I always knew you'd wind up dating your mother," he said.

I was laughing as he walked, then I stopped. "What's that supposed to mean?" I called. Got no answer.

After we'd killed some time in the front yard, playing with Tag, who seemed now like such a smashingly fine dog, fetching Popsicle sticks and chasing his tail and throwing himself on his back when I growled at him, it was time to go.

Barbara unleashed massive doses of home training on my mother, thanking her sweetly and inviting her to her house sometime and generally leaving Ma as weak and stupid as she'd left me. Then, when I was sure that the other guests had safely cleared the area, I told Ma that

I'd be walking Barbara home as planned.

As hoped.

As dreamed.

Ma waved us on out of her yard and saw us to the gate. I looked back at her, and she was very very clearly happy and proud for me. And a little bit, she was something else.

I know, because I felt it for a second myself, whatever it was. But just for a second.

LEAFING

THROUGH

I competed with Tag through the whole walk to Barbara's house. The dog would get tangled up in her feet, making Barbara scold it playfully. So I would cross over in front of her, steering her off the curb into the gutter.

"What's the matter with you? Cut that out," she said to me, not as nicely as she'd spoken to Tag.

We got to the intersection where traffic was moderate for an early fall evening, just as the sun was finally gone and we could hear the streetlights humming to life above us. She scooped up Tag and nuzzled her, explaining to the dog, in a kind of modified baby talk, how dangerous traffic was and how no, no, no, she was never to run in the street.

I scootched up close, my upper arm touching hers, as we waited for the light to change.

I was looking straight ahead, steely and determined as if the only thing in the world that mattered to me was the changing of that traffic light and the safe passage of my little family. When all that *really* mattered to me was the contact I was making with Barbara's arm.

But I could see out of the corner of my eye as she looked at me. At my arm, then up at my grinning, over-heating mug. Tag took the opportunity to lick madly at Barbara's jaw, as if she had on beef gravy perfume. Hey dog, that was going to be *my* move.

"You sure got a houseload of very friendly dogs," she said to me.

I finally faced her head-on. "Oh, and we're just getting started," I said, "wait'll you see."

I cringed as soon as I said it, before Barbara even shoved off the curb toward the opposite sidewalk, leaving me staring into her vacated spot in my universe.

"Oh, I get it," I said as I caught up to her. "You mean, like, I'm a friendly dog too, like, one of those mental, way too friendly dogs? I get it. Well you don't have to worry about that. See . . . I'm not that kind of dog. . . . I mean I'm not one of those . . ."

That was the outside conversation. The inside conversation was going on at an even faster pace, and it sounded more like this:

Shut up, Elvin, shut up, for the love of god shut up. Don't say anything more. Lick her face or her shoes or chase a stick or root through a garbage can but please find something else to do with your mouth other than talk-ing anymore. No good, no good. Danger. Turn around. Run home. No explanation, no forwarding address, just get out while you can. . . .

Barbara held her little dog up in front of her face,

keeping it between herself and me like a shield. "Down boy," she said. To me, not to Tag.

See, we did think alike. I knew it.

"See, we do think alike," I said. "I was just kind of thinking of myself as a dog, and there you were thinking the same thing. Do you get that, that we both think kind of the same?"

Barbara put Tag down, and let her flop along ahead of us. My pulse immediately slowed, and I stopped talking. No, wait, it raced. Then I *resumed* talking.

"Shush," Barbara said, in a friendly cautionary way.

I shushed.

The wind was picking up, making it feel and taste more like fall. Leaves were popping themselves off the trees and laying themselves down ahead of us as we turned the corner onto Barbara's tree-busy street, and Tag was occupied enough chasing the small tornadoes of leaves that blew around from the swirling breezes that we didn't have to control her very much. She really was a good dog after all, wasn't she.

"This is my house," Barbara said, picking Tag up and hugging her. She was, in fact, speaking to Tag more than to me. Fair enough, since this was the dog's new address and not mine.

A light snapped on in the driveway as soon as Barbara pushed on her trellised wooden gate.

"Motion-sensor lights," I said like one of those do-it-yourself doofuses, who love to show you they know every boring home improvement detail.

"Nope," Barbara said. "Girl-Protector lights. Connected on the other end to my dad."

I took a step back from the fence, started looking the house up and down the way you do when you hear a voice but you don't know where it came from.

"That was one of the nicest nights of my life, Elvin," Barbara said, from what seemed like a half mile away. It was probably more like six feet.

"Ya?" I said, then realized I should probably try to not sound surprised. "Uh, ya. My ma can cook, for sure. And it was pretty great to unload all those dogs. I thought we were going to have to . . ." I made the hanging-from-a-noose, tongue-dangling gesture.

Barbara was not impressed. She hummmphed at me before going on. "Your mom is the best. Tell her I said so."

"I tell her all the time," I said, and for once, Barbara and I really *were* saying the same thing at the same time.

As she backed away, toward the house, Barbara made a head gesture up toward wherever her father was hovering behind a curtain. "You understand," she said.

I nodded, even though I didn't entirely understand and didn't much care to. I just watched her go. Sigh.

So disoriented I almost forgot.

The party. Hell. I was not home free yet. I had not done the dangerous part, the asking. The risking.

Quit, I said to myself, and really really meant it. You can't go up from here, Elvin Bishop. You can only trash all the good you've had. Quit, while you're ahead. Quit, while you're crazy happy. Quit, while you can still walk. Just quit, and thereby win, for a change. Quit.

"Quit what?" Barbara asked, tilting her head in puzzlement.

Beautiful puzzlement. Sweet, playful puzzlement, letting her mouth hang a small bit open, hinting that one of us was kind of nuts. One of us *was*, and when he was unable to answer her, she waved and turned to go again.

"Barbara," I said desperately, just as she'd turned the tumblers in the big dead-bolt on her big oak door. Fortunately I think desperation in my voice had become a kind of white noise to her.

She stopped. She waited.

"Okay, there's a party, see . . . and usually frosh aren't invited. In fact Frankie and me are like the first two in history, because we're kind of—"

"Darth's party, right?" she asked. "Sorry to cut you off there, Elvin, but the way you take the long way around things . . . it'll be dawn before I get in the house and I won't be going to any parties for a long time. Anyway, I was at the point where I was worried you were going to take some other girl."

The old nausea of joy rose in my stomach again. Fortunately words failed me once more.

"Now that you know where I live, maybe you could come and pick me up if that's all right. Unless you want me to meet you. . . ."

Of course that was all right, and of course she knew it was all right.

Now!

What the hell was that?

Now. The moment. Now. Be bold for once. *Act.* Now.

"Now *what?*" she asked.

If Barbara was hearing the voice, I had to act quickly or total self-destruction was certainly my next move.

She must have been good and paralyzed by the sight of me marching up her front steps, right there in full view of her father and his floodlights and everything. Because she simply stood there and waited. No comment, no smile, no defensive tae kwon do posture.

I didn't stop till I got there. And when I got there . . .

Yes I did. I kissed her, kissed Barbara, this most prettiest of girls I have ever seen. Even as I was doing it I was worrying it, fearing she would snap out of it and scream me away, but it didn't happen. What happened instead was that she allowed her lips, her pillowy thick lips, to be pressed against mine. And they had, like, muscles to them, under the softness, little twitchy things of movement that I swore were somehow electrified and would shock me to near death.

And so they did.

When the porch light started flicking madly, I figured it was just me. Brain overfiring and all. So that Barbara was already well inside her doorway, waving, by the time I realized I was solo again.

But I was altered then, the pressure off, the aloneness a different thing from what it ever was before. Not altogether alone. And not feeling I had anywhere to get to. I don't think I stood there staring at the house for more than ten minutes. Maybe fifteen.

When I was a kid and I felt good, I used to chase the dried leaves in autumn all over, crazily, as the wind whipped them up and down, circular and straight and fast and without a pattern. It was pure stupid happiness. I'd do it all up and down the street and must have looked completely insane to the neighbors in their windows.

And to Barbara's neighbors as I did it now.

PREP FOR SURGERY

I spent three hours in the bathtub. Stole a fistful of Ma's colored bath oil balls from The Body Shop, broke them open in a steaming, almost unbearable tub full of water, then sat there until I had soaked all the dork out of me. By the time I stood up, pink and wrinkled as a newborn, the bathwater had turned to a thick oily soup. So I followed it with a shower to de-slick myself.

"Smells awfully nice in there," Ma called as she passed outside the door at one point. But that was it. Maybe I was giving off something other than carrot and lemongrass oils, because she kept strangely distant and silent with me all afternoon.

Or maybe it was me who was strangely distant and silent. Because for sure I was spending more time sprucing alone than I had spent at any time since my first penance. And that was only because I had to compose some believable sins to replace the only real ones I had, which I was too embarrassed to discuss even if the priest was in a little dark box and couldn't see me.

No problem with that now, though. Already had the one big whopper sin to contemplate.

Sally. I never fixed what I did. But I was hoping that the whole thing just kind of healed up all by itself. You know the way little kids cover up their eyes and think nobody can see them? That was me. My version of covering up my eyes was having Frankie invite Sally to the party. And when he reported back that she was happy to go and that she seemed to hold no leftover bad feelings . . . well, that meant nobody could see me, right? Maybe the problem just did fade away, right?

Like my hemorrhoids. And all my fat. A good bit of it, anyway. I stood there looking into my mirror, wearing only my underwear and the long grandfather shirt with the million buttons that Mikie and Frankie practically took me by force to buy. I held the shirt up, so I could get a better look at myself, and my self was only lopping over the waistband of my boxers by about an inch, maybe two, rather than the three inches of a while back. I leaned closer to my mirrored self, examining the shirt closer, and me in it. The powder-blue stripe, barely noticeable between the thin-enough brown stripes, over the cream background, that worked. It gave me the look of, almost, robust health. Made me look flesh-colored and lean, as opposed to Michelin Man bumpy, and Michelin Man white, like I was used to looking in another lifetime.

I reached behind me without looking away from the mirror, for fear that the illusion would shatter, that the image would be replaced by . . . you know. I pulled my pants off the bed, those same pants I had bought on that same shopping trip before that first dance. The pants my two friends had gotten me to buy and that my mother had then shrunk, forcing me to perform the great Houdini convulsive snake dance to even fit into.

They slid up over me easily now. Just as if they belonged to me.

I tucked the shirt in. No tent maneuver for this boy.

I stared.

I looked good. I really did. How did that happen? Did somewhere along the line the Army Corps of Engineers come in and do an overhaul of the EB infrastructure? No, it was more than that.

It was Barbara, making me sick enough that I couldn't eat and nervous enough that I ran everyplace I went.

But it was more still.

I watched myself, something like a movie, but more like the outtakes from a movie, as I started dancing a bit in the mirror, hips shaking. Stopping. Shaking again.

I had to laugh at myself. But I didn't mind at all, laughing at myself.

Right. They had done me all right, my boys. They'd really taken me by the hand through this social thing. I'd have to finally say something to them, at the party tonight. It would be kind of cool, like, a *moment*. A real celebration of like, all new stuff happening . . .

Oh.

No. Wait. That wasn't going to happen, was it?

I ran to the phone, dialed one of the few numbers I knew by heart.

"Franko."

"Studley."

"Cut it out, this is serious. I just realized, Mikie's not invited to this party."

"I know that. This kind of thing happens, El. Don't sweat it. Mikie's not sweating it."

"He's not? Really, you talked to him about it?"

"Of course not. Grow up, El, guys don't talk about stuff like this. I know Mikie's not sweating it because Mikie's not a dink, that's all. There will be other parties."

"No."

"There won't? Elvin, you know something I don't?"

"No, I mean, no, can't we not leave Mike out of it? Can't we bring him along?"

"Elvin, what did Darth say to you, exactly? He said you could come, and you could bring a date, right?"

"Right."

"So that is what you can do. That is *all* you can do. There is no messing with the arrangement, trust me on this."

"I believe you, Frank. Your friends are a little freakish about their details, don't you think?"

"Yes. Yes I do think. And I will never mention it to them."

"Then *you* get him invited, Frank."

"Elvin?" Frankie's voice came out all strange and unrecognizable to me. High, like I hadn't heard it sound since first grade. "Listen, I don't want to go places Mikie can't go. And probably I could figure out a way to get him there. But you know what? Mikie ain't like you or me. You want to *really* make him feel bad? Treat him like a lame-o who has to get a charity invite to a party. *This* he can deal with. *That* he couldn't."

"So, what would happen if I just brought him anyway?"

Frankie sounded so sad, and scared for me when he then said, "Oh, Elvin," it was almost as if I was already hospitalized, surrounded by flowers and a blurry doctor saying, "Can you feel this then, Elvin? How 'bout here, any feeling here?"

Frankie continued my education. "It isn't done, okay? Just not at all cool. And in his own way, Mikie is very cool. He knows what's what. He doesn't make mistakes."

Hearing what I already knew about Mike just made me more depressed. I sighed. "Maybe I just won't go, then."

"Oh, Elvin," Same sound again. Same intonation. Same hospital.

"What, Frankie, they'll beat me up just for not being there?"

"They're really a lot more sensitive than people give them credit for," Frankie said. And in his world, that made some sense.

Problem was, that's the world I was in at the moment. I considered the implications.

"I don't care what they do to me," I said, my voice quavering because I most certainly *did* care, but this was just what a guy said when he was being brave.

"But you do care what Barbara does," Frank said. "Elvin, listen to me here. Barbara wants to go to this party. You want what Barbara wants. Mikie is your friend, so he wants what you want. Ipso faxo, Mikie wants you to go without him."

I sat silently on my end of the phone. I didn't want to agree with him, because I thought I was a better guy than that. I didn't *want* to agree with him.

So I just shut up.

"So Mike spends tonight at home or whatever," Frank said. "There's always tomorrow. He'll still be Mikie. *I* might die if this party went on without me, but *he* won't. I'll see you at the party." He hung up quickly then, because neither one of us wanted to talk about it one bit further.

He was right, though, right? This party wasn't so special. I was making it a bigger thing than it was. It wasn't like my first penance, it wasn't anything like my first penance.

Right. Because at my first penance, Mikie was right behind me in line, supplying me the sins I needed to get through it.

I dialed the other number I knew by heart.

"Hey," I said.

"Hey," he said.

Silence.

196

"Hey," he said again. "Hold on, somebody wants to talk to you."

I held on as somebody took his time coming to the phone. Then, there was a sound, like an obscene phone call, only the caller wasn't having any fun at all. There was the heavy breathing, followed by a lot of desperate gnashing of teeth and chewing of the phone receiver, and weird little coughs like the speaker had swallowed the phone cord and only gagged part of it back up.

"She's an excellent dog," Mikie said.

I started laughing. "Is she sick?"

"Nope. Just excited."

"Excited? How'd you manage that? I could barely detect a pulse. When she was born, I had her all wrapped up in newspaper ready for burial until she squiggled out and started suckling one of my bike tires."

"I let her watch TV," Mike said. "It stimulates her. She's my new couch buddy."

Zing. I was his old couch buddy.

Another pause. I was usually more words and fewer pauses, so I was not firing on all eight here.

"Great dinner," Mike said finally. "I mailed your mom a thank-you—seeing as she was the one who invited us and all."

"Great home training."

"I know it."

More pause. God I hated that.

"Barbara's pretty great," he said. "I'm jealous as hell."

"Shut up," I said. To my knowledge, no one had ever

been jealous of me in my whole life. Except maybe for the *real* losers, and Mikie wasn't one of those.

"Okay," he said, with a laugh, "I'll shut up."

The TV went on in the background. "The dog did that," Mikie said. And I knew we were not going to talk about *it*. But hell, I kissed a girl, in front of her father even. I could try this.

"What's gone wrong, Mike? Something's not right. I should be home tonight. You should be smoothing away at the party. That would make sense. That would be—"

"I don't mind looking like the leave-him-home loser," he said.

"That's 'cause you've never *been* that," I said. "Sure, you don't mind. *I* mind. I can't feel right. I'm having troubles here. You should be the guy invited, the guy with the girlfriend. You should be—"

"You know what, El?" Mike said, calmly serious now. "I shouldn't be. And you should. I don't *want* to be at this party. If they did invite me, I wouldn't even go."

I was about to give him Frankie's speech about when these people invite you, you *go*, whether you like it or . . . then I realized: No, Mikie wouldn't.

"And I don't want a girlfriend. I might. Tomorrow maybe. Don't right this minute though. Whadya think, El . . . that okay?"

Is that okay? Sheesh . . . Was it what I thought he'd say? Well, no. But was it okay?

It was Mikie who said it, right?

"Duh," I said.

198

We both knew to stop then. That much was the same—we knew when to shut up on each other.

"So I'll see ya then," he said. "You gotta go."

"Oh." I gotta go, well I suppose. I'm ready to go, I'm not sure at all about that. "Okay, I'll see ya, then, Mike."

"Have an excellent time," Mike said, and clearly, he meant it. Because Frankie was right, Mike was no dink.

He was *so* not a dink.

When I reached Barbara's, she was in her front yard. She was not at all sweaty, as if she did this kind of high-grade social stuff all the time. Standing a few feet in front of the house, wearing calf-high paint-splattered boots, a quilt-pattern skirt of mostly denim and orange velvet patches, and a black T-shirt with an eagle on the front that was so massive its wing tips wrapped around and hugged her in back. She was bouncing a neon-green tennis ball off the steps.

"You look . . . wow," I said.

"Thanks." Barbara snatched the ball out of the air off the last carom and flipped it up onto a wicker love seat on the porch.

I was looking the house up and down, as if I were thinking about buying it.

"He's not here," she said, picking up her white denim jacket, then nudging me on out of the yard. "They went out."

"Oh," I said, and I suppose sounded a little more excited than I should have.

"They didn't go out for*ever*, Elvin," she said. "Just for a little while. They will be back way before the party is over."

"Oh," I said, much more calmly. "Didn't they want to meet me, check me out or anything?"

"Nah, after my dad saw you out there chasing leaves, he said there was no hurry."

Ouch. "He saw that, huh?"

She smiled, looking straight ahead at the open road before us. Well, the open sidewalk. "Yup. He saw it."

You know the way you say something to somebody, it's half a question and half a command, as if you can force the answer to be what you want it to be? "You didn't see it though."

While continuing to walk, Barbara turned her head my way. "I think it's good to be childlike."

We can assume she saw.

"Well anyway, that means, that's good, right? With your father, that is. He likes me then, right?"

"Oh sure. When he stopped laughing, he told me he wished *all* my boyfriends were eleven years old. He'd sleep better."

My mind worked that one over frantically, trying to find something good. "He likes my boyish quality."

"Bingo," she said brightly. I think she was trying to help me out.

But then the other part kicked in. What did her father mean, *all* her boyfriends?

PARTY ON, DARTH

We walked in the door to Darth's fairly lavish home. It was a big old three-story stone place, like a giant cinder block with one of those widow's walk things on top. It had apparently been some sea captain's home originally, and was still decked out in nautical stuff, oak everywhere, barometers and harpoons and ships' wheels and petrified starfish all over the place even though Darth's old man wasn't a sea captain but a car dealer.

"So, she's not talking about it at all, right?" I whispered in Frank's ear. "Her damaged rep and all that?" There was no one close enough to hear us, but it was the kind of place where you felt like you were being monitored.

"Come on," Frank said. "She's *my* date for a hot party. Her reputation's the last thing on her mind."

This, oddly, brought me great relief. "You're the man, Franko."

He was looking all around the place as if he were in a wax museum with all his heroes in it. "No I'm not,"

Frank answered. He gestured at all the stuff, the piano, at the framed photos in the entryway of Darth's dad arm in arm with very important-looking people we did not know but who must have been *somebody*. "No, I'm not the man. This is the man." He went right up to the pictures, got close enough to one to fog the glass. He wiped it off again. "I think this guy in this picture is like, a TV news guy or something."

I looked closer, just to be polite. "He does the weather before school in the morning."

Frankie leaned away, tapped the glass of the picture. "That's what I want, right there. Power, fame, style."

I couldn't relate. What I wanted was a lot simpler.

I went to find Barbara, who had gone with Sally to scope out the snacks and beverages situation. Remarkable, no? Two girls from entirely different social circles, united by their relationships to me.

Gasp, there it is again. Relationships, with girls. Plural, even.

I located them in the dining room, where the ten-foot table was laid out with a very professional-looking buffet of small sandwiches, shrimp on toothpicks, white-corn tortilla chips, guacamole and salsa and sour cream, crackers, Muenster cheese, soft spreadable cheese, cheddar cheese so sharp it'd make you bleed. There were a couple of cold noodle dishes, Thai peanut and sesame, along with thin finger-length raw veggies and dips of such intense colors that either somebody picked them out of an organic garden fifteen minutes ago or somebody had painted them. Guava juice, pineapple juice, Italian sparkling water, real root beer with pieces of root in it for good measure, many different bottles of wine with labels that had no English on them, standing behind tall cut-glass goblets that were so fancy you could swear they danced when the music from the basement rumbled the table. There was an ice bucket big enough to fit my head in standing guard beside the table in its own six silver legs.

"Good evening," Darth said from behind the four of us. We must have been gawking so obviously that it showed on the backs of our heads. "Don't be shy. It's there to be eaten."

"Whoa," Frankie said, shaking Darth's hand very hard the way a salesman does in the appliance store before he realizes you don't want a stereo, just some blank cassettes.

"Whoa yourself," Darth said, shaking Frank, shaking him *off*, and walking right up to the girls. Skipping me altogether.

"Sally, right?" Darth asked, and he pointed at her in an I'll-get-back-to-you-in-a-second manner.

"Yes, hi," Sally answered. She seemed flattered that he already knew her.

"I don't know you though," he said to Barbara, whose hand he took and held lightly while she spoke.

"Barbara," she said. "Thanks for having us to your party."

"No, thank you for coming. If it wasn't for girls like

you and Sally, I'd be stuck looking at people like these guys"—he thumbed toward us—"all night. And that would make for an aesthetically bad party."

"Oh, I don't know," Barbara answered, looking me and Frankie over with a nod. "I think they make nice party decorations."

Darth made his way to Sally, took her hand lightly the way he had Barbara's. With very little pause he nodded at her, bent like a gent, and kissed the back of her hand.

I swear I saw his mouth open when it was on the back of her hand. I swear it. Not that I was, you know, obsessing over it.

I figured on some fireworks now. Sally can get pretty steamed. . . .

She smiled. She nodded.

"Wine?" he asked. Then he passed his look over the rest of us, spreading the invitation over us like peanut butter rather than repeating it three more times.

"Well, I don't . . ." Barbara began.

"Well, I do," Sally said.

"Make it two," Frankie said.

I waited, to see what Barbara would do. Darth did not.

"Oh sure you will," he said. "I'll have one with you. Red or white?"

Pauses all around.

"Red it is," Darth announced, and proceeded to pour. He half filled five of those sparkly glasses with ruby-looking wine, then delivered, two by two, ladies first, of course, before lifting his own. "Welcome to my home," he said, and we all clinked glasses with him very, very carefully.

After enduring my tiny sip of surely outstanding wine, I snatched a quick look all around. Yup, everybody but Darth was making the same I-just-drank-pickle-juice face.

"Come on down to where the actual party is going on," Darth said, walking out and motioning for us to follow.

That was a relief. I had begun to wonder if there was a party here at all, or if we had been lured to one of those suave murder-mystery parties where rich people actually kill somebody out of boredom. I'd seen only one other person there, and she simply fixed herself a small plate of cheeses and broccoli trees and disappeared again, down the cellar stairs where we were now walking.

The music got louder, got thumpier as we got closer to the source. The source, in the end, was a very large entertainment-complex thing, with a television screen covering one entire wall, dark wood furniture and low lights giving the place a warm feel even though the wide-open rectangular room was nearly as long as a basketball court. The music poured out of surprisingly small speakers. Thirty surprisingly small speakers, ringing the room like high-security TV cameras, high up on the walls.

None of this was what I'd expected. I thought there would be a certain amount of rowdiness, perhaps some visible flesh, bawdy drinking songs, Ibiza dance videos, and deafening savage music.

The music was some kind of jazz that had a beat in there someplace, but sounded more like a bunch of different instruments playing different songs with great seriousness. The silent monster of a television flashed some Eurosport channel with a bunch of sports nobody really played like hurling and curling and bocce ball. Even the people there—including Obie and all the scary members of the Photography Club—were strangely quiet and within the law, sitting on the leather sofas, talking quieter than the music, and using coasters.

"Excuse me," Darth said, suddenly agitated. He ran to a corner of the room, far from the TV and stereo action, where it didn't even seem he'd been looking.

"Is that a spill?" he asked a shocked couple. "On the floor, right there, is that cocktail sauce I'm looking at?"

I covered my mouth as I started laughing. Barbara did the same. Frankie came up close behind me. "Is this awesome, or what?"

I turned just my head, like an owl, to see him. "Awesome is one word for it," I said. "*Boring* is another."

"What are you, nuts?"

"Franko, there is nothing going on here. It's like a school field trip to Old Sturbridge Village when it's closed."

"Once again, you are so out of it, El. There's more going on than meets the eye, I'm sure of it. This is probably the setup for some excellent devil-worship ceremony or something, you'll see. Then you'll feel stupid you said that."

"Hey, I feel stupid already, thanks."

Our host was coming back to us, shaking his head sternly.

"Do you think I was too hard on them?" Darth asked. He took a sip of his wine, since the question clearly did not require debate, as he was shaking his head no while asking.

"If you don't mind my prying," Sally pried, "where are your parents?"

"Oh." He brightened. "I slipped them a few bucks and shoved them off to Plum Island."

We all laughed, not because it was a great line—it was just okay—but it becomes pretty clear in these situations when you are *supposed* to laugh.

Sally, however, appeared to mean it. "You're funny," she said.

"Ya, I am." Then, finally, Darth noticed me. He came over and gave me a firm hug around the shoulders. "But the real funnyman is this guy here. Sphinc, you having a good time?"

I nodded. Tough spot here. I was earning some points—getting instant stares from all sectors of the room—by appearing to be Darth's only full-contact buddy. But I had to believe I was losing some too, by being the Velveteen Sphincter. What do you think?

"Funniest guy in the school, right here," he said, slapping me on the chest with his free hand.

"I know it," Barbara said. She smiled at me proudly, which added inches to my height, and my chest. "He gets it from his mother," she added, before excusing herself to the bathroom. Sally went with her.

"What a coincidence," Darth said when they were just out of earshot. "I get it from his mother too." He slapped me on the chest again.

I saw Frankie stiffen. We were both a little possessive of my mother. However, only one of us was mentally imbalanced on the subject. I whacked Darth right back, in the chest.

It felt like I had struck a sheet of marble behind a silk curtain.

Darth remained unruffled. "Yo, Sphinc," he said calmly. "I cured your 'rhoids; I can give 'em back to ya even quicker, know what I mean?"

Did I know what he meant? In the time it took him to make that statement, the affliction *came* back, with the stress.

How does he do that? Go from Señor Smoothie to Joe Knuckles just like that? Spooky, is what it is.

The girls returned.

"You know," Darth mused, "this is why I have parties. I feel like a different person altogether, when there are beautiful ladies around. The world is a better place."

Ah-hah.

"You know," he added, "that our school is full of nothing but boys."

Everyone nodded. Like we were at a wake.

"Please excuse me, ladies," Darth said, bowing. "There is hosting to be done." And he saw himself out, out of the room, out of the party, actually, as he went back up the stairs to where nobody seemed to be.

"Now *that* is home training," Barbara said.

I was not about to disagree, because I didn't want it to sound like sour grapes. Ouch.

Fortunately Sally, woman of the world, did the honors. "There's something kind of scary about him though," she said, looking at the hot spot in the air where Darth had just been.

Ah, good. Sanity.

"But in a most intriguing way," she concluded.

Frankie was definitely taking notice, that Darth was catching the eye of his date. But unlike what I would have done—sweat, run around flapping my arms and telling jokes and saying please look at me, not him—he merely seemed to be observing, like an apprentice to a master craftsman.

I was suddenly tired. I led the way to a couch, the last one left, right next to the stereo. It sat across from a matching green leather love seat where Sally and Frankie took up residency. Barbara and I sat across from them, settling deep into the overstuffed, oversoft buttery leather, for some nice four-way conversation. Maybe the evening wouldn't be so bad now after all.

Make that two-way conversation. The smell of

leather or something had an effect on Sally and Frank, but they opted out of the conversation immediately and decided to wrestle instead.

My, the apprentice is a quick study.

Barbara and I, with a much bigger area to use, turned and faced each other on the couch in a more civilized fashion. I would have paid a million dollars if Frankie would trade me that love seat.

"Anyway," I said to Barbara as if we had been talking for hours. "You kind of think Darth's cool I bet, huh?"

She took one more sip off of her wine—her first sip in a long time—grimaced, and set the glass down on the end table near her. Relieved, I passed her my glass too. "I can't finish either," I said.

We both laughed, like kids, looking around at everybody (other than the two persons nearest us) as if we were going to be discovered and asked to leave for not fitting in.

"So," I said, and by now it seemed I *had* been carrying on this conversation for hours. "You kind of like him I guess, huh?"

"Will you stop, Elvin?" she said. "He is interesting, and you can't deny that. But I can see what Sally means, about him being maybe a little spooky."

Just at that moment, the spooky host returned. He came right toward us, with a silver tray and an obvious sense of purpose. Sort of like before when he scolded the people who spilled, he seemed miffed.

"I'm sorry the wine doesn't agree with you," he said, placing one fresh goblet in Barbara's hand, then one in mine. He took the two glasses off the end table. "I think you'll like this better." And, since he stood there over us, we figured we'd better try.

Fortunately, I didn't have to fake it. "This is the best root beer I have ever tried," I said.

"This is out*rag*eous," Barbara gushed.

Darth nodded, ho-hum, but did let a small smile lash his handsome mean strong bony face. "My father has it imported from Indonesia. Same place I got your ointment," he said.

"Ointment?" Barbara asked.

"Skin condition," I said as Darth walked away.

"Ah," she said, shaking her head in admiration as he left the party again. "He does it all, doesn't he? Now don't take this wrong, Elvin, but I gotta say, he's an amazing guy." She raised her glass to mine before we both sipped. "This is some unbelievable service here."

Sure is, I thought, with a chill. "But he wasn't even in the room. How did he know we didn't like—"

Our heads were turned by a big sucking sound, caused by Frankie removing himself from Sally's face. "It's true, you know. He's like, rich, *and* big and strong and athletic and scary, and he has good manners and stuff. The guy's got everything," Frank piped.

We all had to agree.

"Well, not *everything*," Frank said and reached up to the stereo and pulled down a CD. He tucked it under his arm, looking all around desperately, like a mime shoplifter. "He doesn't have *this*."

We were all laughing. He'd never stolen a thing in his life, and he sure wasn't going to start by ripping off a murderer/role model. But the door to the room swung open, the brighter light of the hallway spilling in and framing Darth in a sort of posthuman glow as he walked grimly our way once more. We all tried to keep our childish little joke to ourselves as Darth stood over us, waiting.

"We're all set, thanks Darth. We haven't finished these drinks yet," Barbara said.

"Put it back," Darth said to Frank.

The smiles were a little easier to keep down now.

"What?" Franko said, looking nervous from his very vulnerable, almost lying-down position on the love seat.

"*Sinatra at The Sands*. It's in your armpit. Please put it back in the CD holder."

Frank was too paralyzed to tell Darth it was just a joke. Or to ask how Darth even knew, for that matter.

Just like that, though, the Man went away, checking around the room for drink orders he might have missed, which of course he had not. Then he was gone again.

"I feel like I'm in an episode of *Scooby Doo*," Barbara said, talking without moving her lips. "He knows every move we make."

"Security cameras," Frank said seriously. "Now that's class."

"Spying on your own guests," I countered. "Now that's *ass*."

We all four tumbled over onto our sides, laughing,

lying there, looking across at each other, hoping that this hid us from surveillance, but probably not. But I looked across and noticed that, with the group flop maneuver we'd done, Sally was leaned over almost completely on Frankie's side, her head resting on his shoulder, her arms wrapped around him. I stared—I guess I do a fair amount of staring—at them, and was warmed by the sight. Somehow I imagined it to be me there, to be us, me and Barbara, and though it wasn't all that much, it was a new high in my fantasy life.

Until I caught Frankie giving me the classic wink-and-nod gesture, calling my attention to Barbara.

Barbara was under me. In the same position, more or less, as the other two. I was so thrilled at that instant, I came one strong heartbeat from losing consciousness completely when she smiled up at me.

Instead, I threw myself off of her, like a proper gentleman, and onto the floor. This made her come right out and laugh. "Can you imagine what this looks like to him, wherever he is? He must think, you know, we're really getting into something here."

"Yar," I said, my brain and tongue both swollen with the idea that she was even speaking the words. "Huh. Yar. Yuf."

But then, we didn't have to ponder long about what exactly old Darth was making of all this. He came back through the door at a trot, and was standing over Barbara—straddling me—before the door closed behind him.

"Hey there, Darth," I said from the space on the floor in between his feet.

"Would you like to take the house tour?" he said, to the ladies. He had a mad determined look on his face, like baboons on the nature program when they are mating while photographers are clicking away and helicopters are buzzing above, red ants are chewing them to pieces and the other male baboons are pelting them with rocks and gourds. Carnal concentration.

"Say Darth, is this linoleum down here, or terracotta?" I asked, as long as he wasn't listening.

"Terra-cotta," he said. "My dad had it shipped from Italy along with the marble in the foyer."

Guess it just depended on what topic you brought up.

"Gee, thanks anyway, Darth," Barbara started saying, but apparently stumbled when it came to giving him a reason why not.

"I'd like to take the house tour," Frankie said.

"Why not?" Darth asked Barbara. Frankie and I did not register at all now.

"I'll go," Sally said. "I love beautiful old houses."

"I'll go if Sally goes," Barbara said, and I sat straight up, worming out from under Darth.

You could say Darth was on a roll.

"Let's, then," Darth said, and held out both arms like an usher at a wedding.

Sally laughed, and held one of the arms with two fingers, like it was electrified, thrilling and life-threatening at the same time. Barbara looked at me.

"Don't mope, for goodness' sake," she said, bopping me on top of the head. "I'll be back in ten minutes."

"Five," I snapped, like I was in charge of *anything*, right?

"Twenty," she snapped back, mocking me.

"Okay, ten."

"Nope. Ten's off the table. Fifteen is the best I can do now."

I must have started doing something awful and embarrassing with my face then, because both Frankie and Barbara reacted.

"Jeez, Elvin, loosen up. She's not going to evaporate on ya," Frank said.

Darth made a big show of checking his watch and breathing loudly.

Barbara reached into the pocket of her pants, pulled out a twenty-dollar bill, and snapped it tight for my inspection. "Elvin, my father gave me this, to take a cab home at any time if you start being weird. Don't make me use it."

She was only half kidding. Less than half, even, she was, like, forty percent kidding.

"Ah, go on," I said, "get out of here." Nice smooth recovery on my part, I thought. But it was a mighty effort. As soon as the three of them had left the room I exhaled, as if I'd been holding my breath for a month.

And the rest of the party guests did the same thing. It was a phenomenon. People started moving, which they really had not done up till then. Guys started nuzzling their girls, standing up, moving to the music to whatever extent possible. Obie—scary mean Obie—came ambling our way with his date. I cringed, but it was okay because he would just be talking to Frankie anyway.

"Way to go, Sphinc," Obie said.

"Huh?"

"Nice work. This'll be good for you."

I looked to Frankie, who shrugged. For once he was not ahead of me.

"The girls. You guys brought the right girls," Obie said, with a heavy dose of *duh* in his voice.

I felt my whole body go rigid, and cold. "What are you saying?"

"What, I'm speakin' Swa-freakin-hili? Darth likes your girls. He's, y'know, like a collector. Loves chicks, like nuts. And he's been waiting for this Sally girl since you gave him the word on her."

My stomach did such a jump there, like something large and live and angry was trying to escape from the inside of me. A feeling I probably should have been having since I told the lie in the first place. *I* had done this. My god, *I* was responsible.

"He likes yours well enough too," Obie grunted on. "It's okay she's a little fat, 'cause she got a really pretty face."

I have never hit anybody in my life. Never even tried. Probably wouldn't do a very good job of it. So there was no reason to expect me to try it.

Must have been my face. Frankie jumped in front of

Obie, and squeezed both of my arms with his hands. "She is *not* fat," I barked. Frank shushed me.

"I guess I need to put on a few pounds before the next party," Obie's girlfriend said, "so I can move up to a better class of loser."

"Can I get you some *punch*?" Obie asked her, making a fist and grinning like a dog snarl. She pretended a big yawn and walked away.

It would be hard to decide *who* to hit in this room once you got started.

"Frank," I said, getting panicky and turning to my only logical source. His face was only inches from mine. I had gotten Sally into a situation. Then Barbara got sucked into the same whirlpool. They were blending together now in my head, both in trouble, both my date, both my *fault*. "Frank, we gotta . . . we gotta, fix it. We have to . . ."

Frankie was frozen. Frankie had been through stuff with these guys before. He probably knew a lot more about them than I did. He clearly had no plan beyond standing there, gripping me. He had been broken.

Maybe it was lucky I didn't know what he knew.

I tore on out of the room and started running up the stairs. Out of the basement I flew right on past the first floor because the kind of stuff I was chasing never happened on the first floor. Second floor, I ran down the hallway, opening every door, without even knocking. Bedrooms, bedrooms—how many people lived here, for crying out loud? Bathrooms. There were three bathrooms on that floor alone. Each room was decorated and draped with thick flowing fabrics hanging everywhere, and one color dominant. A gold room, a forest-green room. It looked like the China Trade Museum Ma dragged me to once. But no Barbara. No Sally. As I thought it, her name squeaked out of me on a breath. "Barbara."

This was silly. This was stupid. This was childish.

It sneaked out of me again as I ran up the third flight. "Barbara."

Third floor, more bedrooms, more bathrooms. A woody study with a desk as big as a coffin, and bookshelves covering each wall. One side crammed with highly polished sports trophies. "Probably bought 'em all," I said, slamming the door.

But no Sally, no Barbara. I ran the length of the thick Indian-looking carpet that covered the hall floor, looking again in all the rooms. Then I stopped, winded, frustrated. Opening and closing my fists and just spending all my energy standing in one spot and fretting.

"The widow's walk." It was Frankie. Couldn't let me go it alone after all. "If it was me, I'd be up on the widow's walk."

"He *is* you," I said. "So he *is* on the widow's walk."

We scrambled again up and down the hallway looking for the stairway until Frankie found it, a mini door, like for little tiny folks, set into the paneling behind the desk chair in the study.

"Boy, could I use a setup like *this*," Frank said, marveling once again at the surroundings.

I blew past him and shot through the little door.

"Take it easy, Elvin," he said. "I mean it, don't go off—"

I was out onto the flat roof before Frankie could finish. And of course I found them there, the three of them.

Barbara and Sally were crouched, on the bay side of the house, looking through two mounted telescopes. Darth was poised behind them, about four feet back. Viewing . . . *them*. He had his arms folded across his big chest, and a large grin splayed across his face. At the sound of my arrival, he turned his look on me, grinning even harder.

"That's *enough*," I said, simply because that was what I had prepared to say.

"What's enough?" Barbara asked, and she sounded agitated.

An excellent question, now that I thought about it.

"What are you two doing here?" Darth said, quietly, but menacingly. "Are you, prowling around my house, uninvited, as if it's a public facility?"

"Come on, El," Frank said quietly, tugging my shirt from behind.

I shook him off. "No," I said, and took a step toward the three. I didn't even know what to say next, what to accuse them of, what to say to explain myself. As a matter of fact, for the instant I saw them up there before I'd broken it up, their thing looked like a not-so-bad alternative to the party itself. Something I would have liked to be invited to instead.

Which, maybe, was the whole problem.

"Yes?" Darth asked. I couldn't tell anymore whether it was that evil politeness thing of his, or if he was simply smart enough to let me hang myself, but he wasn't confronting me.

"I came . . . to help," I said, making sense I suppose to nobody who was not named Elvin. "Thought you'd need . . . help."

Sally let out a little laugh. "I'm a big girl," she said, waving me away. "In fact, we're both big girls."

"Big girls," Darth echoed.

"You know, guys," Sally said, gesturing toward the telescopes, "no offense, but I can look at you anytime, but ordinarily it's a twenty-five-minute drive *with* my family to catch the ocean. You understand." And with that, Sally went back to seeing the sights.

Darth did likewise, taking two steps closer to the backside of Sally. "Please take the most direct route back to the basement—or out the front door," he said without looking at us.

"Well," Frankie said, clapping his hands and rubbing them together, "that was clear enough." He started down.

I risked the walk toward Barbara.

As I approached her, she took the twenty out of her pocket and held it like a flag, flapping hard in the stiff rooftop wind.

Thirty percent joking. And falling.

When I got close, I did the best I could do for an explanation.

"I really like you a lot," I whispered.

She nodded, put the bill back in her pocket. "Try to like me a little less," she said. "I'll see you downstairs."

It was breezier, it was chillier up on that roof than I had realized. My face felt wind-whipped and numb as I descended. My hands felt the same way.

I tried, walking alone, to take Barbara's advice. Tried to like her less. Not because I wanted to, and not because any part of me believed I was capable, but because I suspected it was going to be very important that I do.

My feet made such a consistent dull *thump thump*ing as I stepped from one stair to one landing to one stair to another over the series of obscenely thick and ornate carpets, the sound could just as well have been made by my heart. And with each step I hammered myself with the thought, *less, less, less, less.*

There were a lot of steps between the roof and the basement of that house.

By the time I reached the sofa near the stereo near *Sinatra at The Sands*, and my friend Frankie, I knew I didn't have a chance of *less.*

It was already somehow *more.*

"You gotta calm down," Frank said, coming across to take the spot on the couch that Barbara had left. "You're too heated up. Trust me, that doesn't play well. Okay?"

he asked, sounding really concerned and really inter-ested in whether or not I got the message. It was as if I was slumped on my stool in the corner and he was saying "Keep your left up, use the jab, keep moving, or you're gonna get creamed."

"Okay," I said. This was so hard for me. Harder than it was for Frankie, that's for way sure. Frankie had the natural fighter's instincts. I . . . I don't know *what* I had.

I wondered, just then, what Mikie had. I could handle this a lot better if Mikie were here.

But he wasn't, and I didn't.

I bolted up out of my seat. Frank made one grab—I broke it like an open-field tackle. "I'm not chasing after you this time, El."

"So don't."

It was a lot quicker this trip, since I knew the route so well. I burst once again out onto the roof, and broke up once again an innocent-looking telescoping party. Innocent-looking to the naked eye, that is. There were also now a bottle of champagne and three bubbling glasses on the ledge.

But no wishy-washy from me this time. I rushed up to Barbara, took her by the hand, and started leading her out.

"Hey Elvin, man, you're getting less funny all the time," Darth said. "I think you better go back—"

"Thanks for the swell time," I said.

Barbara shook out of my hand—aggressively.

"What?" I asked. "Barbara, trust me, he's really not a good guy."

"What gives you the right . . ."

She was actually walking back—to Darth. Grinning Darth.

I followed. "Because . . . it's the right thing . . . I'm doing what's right," I said, as if I had a clue anymore what was the right thing to do. As if I ever did.

Sally swung her telescope around to peer at me. "You're embarrassing everybody, you know. Not to mention being a big fat dud."

"I am not f—" I caught myself, realizing what was *not* the point here.

"But you *are* embarrassing me, Elvin," Barbara stage-whispered.

I grabbed her hand once more. I pleaded. "Please . . . I'm sorry . . . I don't know what I'm doing . . . we can talk. Can we. Come on, we can."

I was cut short, literally, by a big hand yanking the back of my shirt. At the same time, Barbara broke free and bolted. Now she was gone and *I* was dangerously trapped on the roof with Darth.

"Now look what you did," he said into my ear so Sally could not hear.

"No, no, you're not going to fight, are you?" Sally said. "Darth, don't—"

"Course not," he said, then went back to my private lecture. "Now I'm left with just the one. But she comes with your highest recommendation. Don't she?"

Has anyone ever deserved a thousand deaths more than me?

"Darth, really now," Sally said, sensing the menace she could not quite hear. "That's enough." And she actually started marching our way. Saving me.

Darth let go and gave me a stiff slap on the back, playful-mean. "Okay, Sally," he said. "Come, let's go finish our drink."

He took two steps toward the champagne.

"I never touched her!" I blurted.

He was back facing me. "What?"

"Never even held her hand!" I was walking backward, toward the door, but still, this was an improvement on my regular cowardice, no?

"What are you talking about?" Sally demanded.

"It's not your business, Sally," Darth said, walking slowly my way. "Just wait over by the telescopes."

"Excuse me?" She was not too pleased, champagne or no champagne.

"I'm telling him you didn't give me VD," I said.

"*Now?*" she shrieked. "Now? A little . . . *slow*, aren't you, Elvin?"

"Really, you and I will settle this in a minute," Darth said to her. "And *slow* won't be a problem. Unless you like it that way."

"Ah, no," she answered knowingly, "I think we're already settled." She brushed past him, fairly banged into me on her way out, saying, "C'mon, you."

Well, it wasn't exactly sweeping me off my feet, but it would do. I followed her out.

"Fine," Darth said, too cool to chase either one of us.

"Go on. And Elvin"—he paused, I did not—"we'll talk."

A lot more chilling a sentence than it sounds.

I trotted down the stairs, first behind Sally, then beside her, then ahead of her. "I'm sorry," I said.

"Ya," she said.

"But, um . . ."

"You better run if you want to catch her . . . and before I start thinking again about what you did."

"Thanks," I said, nervously. "I bet you'll still be able to catch Frankie too."

"Catch Frankie?" Sally laughed. "That'll be a switch."

She was waiting in front of the house for her cab.

"I can walk you," I said.

"It's dark," she said.

"You'll have me to protect you."

"And who to protect me from you?"

"Come on, Barbara." I was sweating, like the old days. I was pacing. My heart was no longer even beating, it was thrashing.

"Listen," she said, "my dad gave me this money to take a cab in the event you started being weird. I think this qualifies."

"But I'm really not . . . okay, I'm weird, sort of, in some ways, but not like—"

I stopped and gasped, nearly choked up, when a cab drew near. When it continued past, I went on, talking faster, aware of my chance speeding away. "I'm not a weirdo like that, really. It's just that I . . . I couldn't deal with . . . I didn't know how to . . ."

Barbara stopped me, out of sympathy I guess because I must have been painful to watch. But she stopped me by grabbing my hand, which I took to be a good sign. You don't take the hand of a menace, right?

"I know you're not a weirdo like that, Elvin. I know that you are really sweet."

I stared at her mouth as she talked. That probably wouldn't help things, but I was powerless. The thickness of her lips.

"But I also don't think you're ready for this. You don't know how to act. You make me nervous. Your reactions to everything are so *extreme*."

She stared at me now, and whatever she saw, I felt embarrassed because I knew I was just proving her point.

"Maybe another time," she said. And this time I was almost relieved when the real cab pulled up. "You just like me too much," she said before opening the car door. She shook her head, as if I would understand it then.

"I really never knew," I said, "that liking somebody too much could ever be a bad thing."

Then I opened her cab door for her.

"Awesome home training," she said, slapping my hand in a nice way as she jumped in.

And as soon as the door was closed, I started running. Like a little kid. I ran and ran and ran and ran and ran home. No zigzags, no circles in the leaves. Straight line. Home.

BLAME IT ON THE DOGS

Ma was sort of hovering for me in the kitchen when I came home that night, though she was good enough to make like she wasn't. When she saw me, she was bright and anxious and happy.

For about a second.

"Can I make you something to eat?" It was her way of feeling sorry for me in a way we could both live with.

Not tonight though. I shook my head and slunk away to my room.

And not the next morning either.

"Can I make you something to eat?" she asked, still hovering, still brandishing the comfort of food. She was still dressed the same way, royal-blue bathrobe over pale-green flannel nightgown, moccasin-style slippers. She could have stayed up all night, just parked herself in that kitchen, ready to take care of me in need like my own personal National Guard. More likely she just slept a little less than I did, and returned to her post.

She was the best. Which was just what I did not want then.

"No thanks," I said. "I'm gonna be out with the dogs."

That definitely raised an eyebrow. But that was all. Ma acted as if everything was like always, as I made my way across the kitchen. Then my brave-little-man routine caught up to me as I reached the refrigerator. I hadn't eaten in what felt like days.

"Well," I said coolly, "maybe I'll take a little something with me."

She watched me, with a relieved small smile, as I cracked the fridge open. I turned on her. "Could you look the other way for a minute?"

"Sorry," she said.

As she turned, I scooped an armload. A whole pack of American cheese slices, a chunk of salami that must have weighed three quarters of a pound, and even Ma's secret little can of chocolate creme ready frosting that she saves in the vegetable bin for watching sad movies. If the "calories from fat" section on the label didn't read at least 80, I wasn't having it.

"You can look now," I said just as I was closing the back door.

I sat with the food, and the dogs, replaying it all just as if I had a commemorative tape of my foolishness. Barbara was so right. When was I going to grow up? I unwrapped the cheese. One slice for mama dog, one for Elvin dog. One half slice for Fusilli-face puppy, one half for Corkscrew, one for Elvin.

228

"Yo, don't bogart that cheese," came the voice from above. Above being the one-foot-by-one-foot square of windowless window on the back wall of the garage. I looked up to the spot to see Mikie's pup, Tortellini, standing there on her two hind legs. Apparently with some help.

Tortellini filled the rotted wooden frame of the window nicely. She looked at me. That is, her face looked at me while her eyes looked at the ceiling. She pointed one paw at me while the other rested, human-like, sort of on her hip.

"Hey you."

"Shut up," I said, and looked down to concentrate on my eating.

"No really"—desperate hoarse whisper now—"Pssst."

And because I am a sap, I looked.

"Have a look at these," the dog said. "Whoppers. They're killing me. I hear you've got the *stuff*. Go on, slather me, slather me. . . ."

And because I had very little else left, I laughed.

"Good. Now gimme a piece of cheese," he said.

I got up and crossed the floor, and held out a slice of cheese, once the dog had gotten herself into a dining position. I leaned against the wall underneath the high window. With one hand I reached up and fed her the cheese. With the other I fed myself.

"Glad you're here," I said.

She turned her rear to me, but this time dog-greeting style. "Ah go on, gimme a sniff. You know you want to."

229

"Mikie," I said, sort of snapped, really.

"Damn, you knew it was me."

"Mike. I got a whole new hurt problem this morning, Mike. And it feels worse than all the old ones combined."

He waited.

"I'm not coming out of here today." I said. "Not all day."

"You want me coming in?" he asked.

"Maybe. What if I start to bawl? Then what would we do?"

"Hmm. Then you just grab up one of us ugly pups and hold it to your eyes. We're just like onions, you know. We'll make like that's what it is, blame it on the dogs."

I liked it. That would do.

"Well, am I coming in, or what, El?"

"Okay, but you have to promise not to make fun of me."

A loud sigh.

"Don't be stupid, Elvin. What else would I want to come in there *for*? Open the door, butt-boy."

I opened the door.